Note From the Author

How do the words love and trust make you feel?
Commitment? How about thick, wet and sticky? Can
words be used to make your pussy moist? Your dick
erect? Your forehead sweat? Can I tell you about a
girl making love to a grown woman and you visualize
every bead of sweat and stain on the sheets as if they
are engaging in intercourse right in front of you? I can
do that. Think I can't? You have secrets you have
never uttered to anyone. Things you replay over and
over in your mind. Inside this book, I have revealed all
of those secrets. The thirst for an orgasm. The hunger
for sexual interaction. Everything you have ever craved
and yearned for is here. Can I get you wet? Can I get
you to rise to this occasion? I bet I can.

~Zion

Once Upon A

FLING

A Modern Un-Fairy Tale

Zion

Second Edition

ISBN: 978-1-940097-32-9
      978-1-940097-31-2
Library of Congress Control Number: 2013952212

Printed in the United States of America

This novel is a work of fiction. Any resemblances to real people, living or dead, actual events, establishments, organizations, or locales are intended to give the fiction a sense of reality. Other names, characters, places, and incidents are either products of the author's imagination or are used fictitiously.

Cover Design by Firstborn Designs, www.firstborndesigns.com

Scarlet

I laid on my back while he did his business on top of me. I stared at my stuffed animals and counted them. Eight. Nine. Ten. When he began to grunt harder, I knew it was almost over. One. Two. Three. Then, he let out a loud groan, and I could feel my insides fill with his nastiness.

"Now, did you have fun playing our game?" he asked.

I just looked at Mr. Happy, my favorite bear. His smile made this not as bad.

"What are the rules, Scarlet?"

I just looked at Mr. Happy, ignoring the question.

James picked me up and held me in the air. Then, he said, "Don't ignore me, little girl!"

With my eyes still on Mr. Happy, I said, "Don't tell Mommy."

"That's right."

He put me down on the bed and walked away. I was ten then. It had started when I was eight: the looks from Mom's boyfriends. Then, at nine, the "accidental" touching. And, at ten, I was old enough to play with. It got worse at thirteen. I had started puberty, and my breasts were coming in, and Mom's new boyfriend Marcos couldn't keep his hands off me.

At first, he would only do it when Mom wasn't home. Then, he would do it when he thought she was asleep. He would be watching television, and I'd be in my room, praying that he wouldn't come in. After my mother said her good nights, I'd listen for her bedroom door to close. Then, I would stare at my clock so hard that I don't think I blinked. And, exactly ten minutes later, I would hear Marcos walk to Mommy's door, listen for a while, and then walk down the hall to my room.

One day in school, someone came to our class and talked about being molested and raped and told us who we should talk to if it happened to us.

"Molly, what do you like to do for fun?" Ms. Hill asked a puppet she was holding.

"I like to ride my bike," the puppet said.

"Oh, I like to ride my bike, too. Who rides the bike with you?"

"Um, Mr. Brown helps me ride."

"Oh, really? Who is Mr. Brown?"

"He's my neighbor. Sometimes, he lets me come to his house, and we play games."

"What sort of games?"

"He said I'm not supposed to talk about it."

"Molly, if any adult tells you not to tell your parents about something, it's usually wrong."

I had known all along that what the men were doing was wrong, but I had never thought of telling anybody. I guess, I assumed I would have been embarrassed. But, one day, I made the mistake of telling Mom about the men.

"Ma, I need to talk to you."

"What is it?"

She was cooking in our small two-bedroom apartment. We stayed in an apartment complex in Chesapeake called the Rivers. Well, it's the Rivers now. Back then, it was called Harbor North. I sat at the table and watched her cook her delicious crab cakes.

"Well, it's about Marcos," I said.

She stopped cooking and said, "Excuse me?"

"Well, he touches me and...does things to me."

"No, that's not true." She nervously opened some cabinets and closed them.

I started crying. "Ma!"

"No!"

"Ma!"

"What are you saying, Scarlet? Huh? The bastard I have feelings for is touching you? Has raped my baby?" She shook her head. "No, I can't believe that. Look at me, Scarlet!"

She struck a pose in the middle of the kitchen floor. She had just gotten off work, taken a shower, and was wearing a loose-fitting satin nightgown and some fresh white socks. She had on no bra, and her breasts were sitting up, real perky. Every little boy and grown man thought she was fine. She had medium-length hair that was cut in a bob, and she never wore makeup because she was just naturally beautiful. "I'm a grown-ass woman! And I'm fine as hell! You're a baby. What would he want with you?"

"Well, it wasn't just him. I mean, every boyfriend you've ever had has touched me ever since I was eight."

Her eyes got wide, and I heard the door close behind me. It was Marcos.

"Hey, baby! You got it smelling good in here."

Mama smiled. "Baby, sit down. I was just fixin' you a plate."

He sat and looked at me. "Scarlet, what you doing in here? You know I don't like looking at kids while I eat."

I looked at my mother.

"Go on to your room."

"But—"

"Scarlet, don't sass me! Go to your room!"

I ran to my room and slammed the door.

"And you better not slam no more doors in this house either!" Marcos yelled after me.

I started crying, really boo hoo-ing. How could Mama take his side over mine? I wondered. Then, as I was contemplating hopping out the window, I heard Marcos scream bloody murder. I ran out of my room and into the hall and saw Marcos on the ground, covered in burning hot oil.

"Nigga, I cook fa yo' ass and take care of yo' broke ass, and you up in my house touchin' and rapin' my damn daughter?" Mama was yelling and cursing and waving the cast iron skillet in the air. She was clearly possessed with all the anger a mother would have at that moment. "I'm gon' kill you, nigga!"

She waved that skillet in the air, and, at the age of thirteen, I watched Mama beat Marcos's head over and over again. It had to have happened fast, but I can only remember it in slow motion.

The first swing was the hardest to watch, that first spray of blood hit Mama's nightgown. The third swing was the most gruesome because her hand slipped, and the skillet actually flew sideways and into Marcos's face. He stopped trying to cover up after that blow, and I think he was officially dead after the fifth one. But Mama wasn't done with him for another two minutes. With every blow she sent his way, more blood shot out of his head and soaked the carpet, the walls, the kitchen table, the kitchen, and even Mama.

Somebody had called the police, and, when the cops came to the door, Mama answered.

4

"Hello, officer," she said, out of breath, soaked in the rain of blood that had come over her.

I don't think there was any lavender left on the front of that nightgown, and there sure wasn't any more brown left on her face. The only things that could assure them she was black were her brown legs. The police looked at her, saw the now-faceless Marcos, and saw me in the background, standing there, wide-eyed. There was no need to ask questions. My mother was taken into custody, and Social Services was called for me.

I think I was still in shock because I had no emotion until that lady came in the house and stooped down in front of me while I sat on my bed.

"Hello, Scarlet."

I just looked at her.

"My name is Ms. Turner, and I'm going to take you to a safe place."

She extended her hand, and, after staring at it for some time, I took it. She led me from my room at the back of the hall, through the blood-soaked living room, and out the front door.

I saw Mama sitting in the back of that cop car and the neighbors standing on their porches, looking at me and whispering, and that was when it hit me. This wasn't going to be good. Mama and I weren't going to the same place.

"No! No!" I yelled as I let go of the social worker's hand and ran toward the cop car.

I was almost within arm's reach of the car when a cop scooped me up and carried me toward a black Lincoln Town Car.

I was screaming, "Put me down! Let me go!"

As I kicked and screamed, I could see Mama trying to get out of the car. Eventually, the officer couldn't hold me anymore, and, as soon as my feet hit the ground, I ran toward the car. As soon as my hand gripped the car door, I opened it and threw my body onto Mama's.

"Mama! Please! Don't let them take you! You were protecting me. Tell them that."

My mother whispered so softly in my ear, "Scarlet, I may not have been the best mama. And, by working so much, I allowed these men to do things to you that are unforgiveable. But you are strong, and, one day, you'll be a better mother than I ever was."

That night, I lost my mother, and, to this day, I believe it was entirely my fault. Unfortunately, the older I got, the more I forgot what she looked like. That has been the hardest part, trying to remember someone you loved so much, yet being unable to. The only picture I had of her was from a newspaper clipping I found, and I didn't want to remember my mother like that.

I think I started fighting and acting out when I got to my first foster mother, Mrs. Rainey. She was a short white woman, who was in her late forties. She had brown hair and itty bitty liver spots on her hands.

I don't even know why she adopted me; she and her house were not designed for children. There were porcelain and crystal figurines all over. All of her furniture was bleach-white, and every nightstand, coffee table, and kitchen table was made out of glass. She often looked at me in total disgust.

Mrs. Rainey took me to the doctor when she first received me. She wanted to make sure I wasn't disease-ridden, I guess. The doctor found out I was about thirteen weeks pregnant with a baby boy, and, knowing that I had been raped, Mrs. Rainey demanded I have an abortion.

"No, Mrs. Rainey, please! Let me keep the baby. I don't want to kill him."

"But, honey, who is going to take care of it?"

"I will! Please! Please!" I pleaded.

She laughed. "Hunny, you're only thirteen. You don't know anything about taking care of a baby."

"But you can help me. I promise, as soon as I turn sixteen and get a job, I'll pay you back. Please don't make me kill him."

She kept laughing. "Oh, you are too cute, but you'll thank me later."

So I laid on that table and let that doctor take my child away. I held Mr. Happy the whole time, looking at his smile, hoping he could make this not so bad. But he didn't, and, after that appointment, he went in the nearest trash can. I cried the whole car ride home.

"I don't know why you're crying. Every time you would have seen that thing's face, you would have seen the father, and your life would be nothing but misery."

"It wasn't a thing," I mumbled.

"What?"

"It wasn't a thing or an it! It was a baby, my baby boy that you killed!"

"Oh, please, Scarlet! You were raped by a Latino man! The last thing this world needs is another Latino and black baby running around, robbing liquor stores, and smoking crack cocaine."

She was going forty-five miles an hour when I opened my door and rolled out. The car came to a screeching halt as I laid in the street without moving.

She leaned her head out of the window and yelled, "Oh, my God! Scarlet, are you all right?"

She didn't even get out to see if I was okay. I got up.

"Oh, come get in the car, darling."

I walked back to the car, and, as soon as I got to it, I slapped the shit out of Mrs. Rainey's face.

I smacked her ass twice and then ran away!

*****

My next foster mother was Madeline Lynn. Madeline was a white woman in her early thirties. She had golden blonde hair that came down a little past her shoulders, and her favorite color was pink. Everything in her house was pink and white. The carpet was pink. The walls were white. The drapes were pink. The lamp shades were pink, and everything that you set your eyes on was either entirely pink or pink with a hint of yellow. Madeline loved dressing me up like I was her personal Negro doll. She hated my name, so she had it changed to Margaret.

"What kind of name is Scarlet Waters?" she would proclaim every time she looked at me.

"Well, it's the name my mother gave me, ma'am."

"Your mother, the cold-blooded killer? From now on, you are to be called Margaret."

At school, all the kids joked about me because I had thick, black hair, and Madeline didn't know how to tame black folks' hair. She didn't even buy the right products for me to do my own hair. Madeline would try to curl it like hers or treat it the way she treated hers, and I'd end up going to school looking like Don King.

One day, this little boy said, "Hey, Margaret! Haven't you ever heard of a relaxer?"

I grabbed that boy, pushed him into a locker, and tried to put my fist through his face. I pounded him so hard he went to the hospital, and I went to local juvenile detention center.

8

While I was in, Madeline said she wanted nothing to do with a thug and gave me back to the state.

When I got out, I was adopted by Jack and Brittany Avery. They were what everybody else called a crazy couple. I can't remember exactly at what age I was adopted by them, but I was way past the age that people want to be adopting kids. But that wasn't why Jack and Brittany were crazy. They were crazy because they could see no wrong in people. They were always smiling and being positive, and, when I was in the midst of it, it just creeped me out. And the way they dressed and lived, it was like the definition of the American Dream.

They owned a white house with black shutters and a red door with a white picket fence. Jack only wore khaki pants and sweater vests when he wasn't dressed in a suit, and Brittany always wore a summer dress. Jack's brown hair was always neatly combed to one side, and Brittany's blonde hair was always done up in curls. I remember, one day, Brittany called me down for dinner.

"Margaret! Margaret, dinner!"

I didn't move.

"Margaret! You coming, darling?"

I still didn't answer.

Finally, Jack came in my room.

"What's the matter, sport?"

"My name's not Margaret."

"It's not? Well, that's the name on your birth certi—"

"No, it's not! My name is Scarlet Waters. I was born in Chesapeake General Hospital on January 18, 1990. My last foster mother thought Scarlet Waters was a stupid name, so she changed it to Margaret Lynn. And I'm not your sport."

He laughed. "Well, there's no need for wind in your jaws. I think Scarlet is a beautiful name. I like the last name

Waters, too. Who was this woman that took that name from you? That's the only thing you have to remember your mama by." He smiled at me. "C'mon. Let's go eat, Scarlet." He stretched his hand out, and I took it.

I had gotten into another fight in school, just because, and, the next day, Jack signed me up for boxing at a gym.

"Now, we can't have you beating up everybody that pisses you off, Scarlet, so we're going to sign you up for boxing."

"I don't wanna box, Jack."

He laughed. "Oh, Scarlet! Here, you can beat up people and get paid for it."

Well, needless to say, I was the best boxer in the gym. Jack ordered this really expensive trophy case and put it in the house.

"Now, Scarlet, it's your job to fill that case up."

And that was exactly what I did. I filled the case and had plaques and pictures on the wall, and Jack and Brittany came to every competition. But my whole life changed the night I lost the championship meet. It was the first match I had lost, and I was in the hospital room crying, not because of the broken nose or the broken arm, but because I felt like I had let them down.

But Jack just laughed. "You're not a loser, Scarlet. You're a loser when you don't try. You tried and succeeded many times. Now that you fell, it's up to you to get back up and fight again."

I smiled, and the two of them hugged me. "I love you guys."

Brittany's mouth dropped. "Oh, Scarlet!"

It was my first time saying it, and I saw a little tear roll down my foster mama's face.

I think that was why I was cool with the gay guy at school. I knew what it was like to be picked on. He couldn't fight for shit, and that was where I came in.

MICHAEL

We were at my father's friend's house in Eva Gardens, and he was showing us his new truck. After we had walked around and got inside, Mr. Joséph, suddenly, said, "You know Cooley's daughter told him she was gay, right?"

"What?" my father yelled.

"Yup."

"And what he say?"

"He kicked her out."

"What? Come on, man! He didn't do that."

"He sho' did."

"You know Bailey's daughter told him she was gay when he got outta prison."

"And what he do?"

"He ain't do nothing. He said he blamed himself 'cause he wasn't in her life while he was, you know, locked up, but—"

My father just shook his head. "I don't wanna know if my kids are gay. Michael!"

I poked my head out from the inside of the truck. "Whaddup?"

"If you gay, don't tell me, hear?"

"Uhhh, I have no intentions of having sex with another guy."

"Good! Still, don't tell me. I don't wanna know!"

I shook my head and sat back on the cool leather of the new truck. I paid my father no mind. He was always talking about something to someone. This was probably the one hundredth time he told me he didn't want to know if I was gay. He had said the same thing to my sister, but I'm pretty sure neither one of us wanted to have sex with someone of the same sex.

My phone buzzed in my pocket. It was a text from my girlfriend.

Marina: "Hey, wyd?"
"Thinking about you," I texted back.
"☺ I love you."
"☺ I know you do. Who wouldn't love me?"
"LOL."

I never told her I loved her. I don't know why. I had love for her. I just didn't love her.

"Mikey!" my father called to me.

I poked my head out of the car door.

"Let's go get us a steak. I'm hungry."

I hopped out of the truck and into my father's car, and we headed to a restaurant. My father loved A-Mayes-N Soul Food on Border Road in Chesapeake. Sheila, the owner, served everything every day. As soon as we walked in, the staff recognized my father.

"Hey!" they all shouted.

"Hey! What y'all doing in here?" my father yelled back.

"What you gon' get today, José?" the lady at the counter asked.

"I want a steak dinner with a side of cabbage and rice. And what you want?" He looked at me. "You want a steak dinner, too? It'll put some hair on your chest." He playfully hit me in my chest, and I fell back a little. "Look at you. You soft. Why don't you get you a steak, man?"

"Why do I have to get a steak? Why can't I get a turkey wing dinner?" I asked, joking around with Pops.

"See, see, soft! Go ahead and tell her what you want."

"I'll have a turkey wing dinner with a side of yams and cabbage and a small side of chitterlings." I made sure I enunciated every syllable in chitterlings, too.

"Why you got to say it like that?"

I laughed. "Is there a problem?"

"Move out the way, faggot." He paid the cashier.

I laughed even harder. Anytime Pops would lose one of our arguments, he called me a faggot.

"Oh, so I'm gay now?"

He looked at me with his big eyes and rolled his neck. "I don't know! Are you? There. Now, answer that."

"Naw, but you might be with all that neck rolling." We moved out of the way, so other people could order.

"Look now," he pointed at me. "I ain't no faggot. I like girls, and they like me."

"Mmm...hmm."

"I got your mama, didn't I?"

"Well, that doesn't prove anything."

We both laughed.

"Yeah, you right," Pops said.

"Yeah, 'cause my mama don't think anybody gay."

"That's for sure."

We sat at a table.

"You know..." Pops hesitated for a bit and looked at his hands. "It's got to hurt some kinda bad knowing that you raised your son to be a man, and he turns out to be gay." He looked up at me. "That's tough."

"Well, I don't have any kids, so I can only imagine."

13

"Yeah, and don't you get no kids 'til you get married—to your wife!"

I laughed. "Pops, I'm not gay!"

"Okay, Michael! Okay! All I'm saying is, if you are, don't tell me."

"But I'm not."

"But, if you ever look at another boy and say, 'Hey, he's a nice-lookin' fella,' don't tell me!"

I laughed and shook my head. "Okay. I'll make sure I never look at a guy that way."

Pops threw his hands up. "That's all I ask."

"Bishop!" somebody from behind the counter called. We both looked, and our food was done.

"Okay, good!" Pops jumped up and ran to the counter. The only time I ever saw my dad run was to go get some food. He came back to the table and handed my plate to me.

"Thanks, fat man."

"Uh huh, this fat man feeding yo lil' hind parts, though."

After we said our grace, we ate like two animals devouring carcasses.

"I tell you one thing. You sure eat like a man." Pops laughed. "You eat like an animal, like a lion." He stretched his arms out across the table, "I present...my son, Simba!"

I just shook my head, and we continued to eat.

Kathryn

We stayed in a three-story townhouse in a neighborhood called Carriage Mill. When you came in the front door, you were immediately greeted by two staircases, one leading down to a restroom, the laundry room, my office, and the garage, and the other leading up to the dining room, restroom, living room, kitchen, den, and patio. At the top of those stairs, another set of stairs awaited, leading to the three bedrooms and two baths. It was a small, quaint home that I'd grown accustomed to, but I was used to better.

I washed my vibrator off, washed my hands, and went downstairs to my office to attempt to do some work. Married life sucked. If I had known I'd be using a vibrator three times a day, I would have stayed single. It was October, and I hadn't had sex since June, not 'cause he wouldn't give it to me, but because he was too eager to. Confusing? I know. Let me explain.

After marriage, sex was not just sex to me. Sex should be used to express love from a male to a female. So my husband came home every night and expected sex, but he did nothing to get it. He didn't cuddle first or engage in foreplay. He just hopped into bed, stared at the wall for a bit, and then asked, "You horny?"

Please! I know B.O.B., my Battery Operated Boyfriend, doesn't fondle me either, but I expect B.O.B. not to do it. I didn't expect my human husband to not do it. And I actually felt that, if I withdrew sex from him, he would get the hint. Please! He tried every night as if the message wasn't delivered and then just went to sleep like nothing happened! Our marriage was not perfect; in fact, it stunk! He said it was because I was worrisome, treated him like a child, and didn't give him sex. Excuse me? Our marriage shouldn't have been built on sex anyway, and how was I worrisome? I thought he was annoying, too, but, of course, what did I know?

My Latino husband worked as a barber, so he was gone from the time he woke up in the morning till seven at night, eight or nine on the weekends. He preached on Sundays, so he was home by two-thirty, but he was so exhausted; he'd sleep till three in the morning. Then, he'd go downstairs and watch a movie, usually *Transformers*, on surround sound. And I was worrisome? Hmm! But he was the breadwinner, so I tried to keep my complaining to a minimum. I had started a business from home, but it wasn't bringing in as much money as I would have liked it to. My kids were doing their own thing, so, at times, this house was as loud as a graveyard.

Perfect example: on a typical Saturday, José was busy at work, and I didn't exactly have friends like that. Jen was with Fish, and I was in the house, staring blankly at my computer screen. I called José, but it went straight to voicemail. His phone never stayed charged. I called Fish, but there was no answer. Knowing she and my daughter were together, I called Jen, but there was no answer there either. They must have been having fun shopping. I knew they had to be because I had loved hanging out with Fish back in college. Even when she was a freshman, she was always the life of the party. And she was an alcoholic. She didn't believe it then and still didn't believe it now. She didn't have to have a drink, but she never knew when to stop. I'll never forget the first time I met her.

I stayed off campus, and I was driving back to the campus to visit a friend. As I drove past my old dorm, there was a thin black girl sitting in a lawn chair in front of the building. She was fanning herself and drinking out of a wine glass. She was completely naked in thirty degree weather at one a.m. I pulled up, took a picture, and was about to back out when something told me to talk to her. I put the car in park, got out, and walked up to her.

"Hey!"

"Hey, Sarah!"

"I'm sorry. I'm not Sarah. My name is Kathryn."

She looked at me with glassy eyes and took a sip from her glass. "Hmm, you look like a Sarah."

"Nobody's ever told me that before."

She took a sip. "Well, I don't know any other white name. You like the name Matilda?"

"No, Kathryn is fine."

She knocked back the last of the contents of her glass, took out a vodka bottle, filled the glass a little over halfway, and poured just enough cranberry juice in the glass to turn the clear liquid red.

"It's thirty degrees out. Why are you out here naked?"

She looked at me as if I was crazy. "Sweetie, it is scorching hot out here. Way too hot for clothes." She took another sip.

"How about we go inside and put some clothes on?"

"Lady, I don't know you! And I know what happens when white people take black people away!" She stood up and gulped down the beverage. "Now, you looka here, you white beast. You think you are better than me, but…"

I couldn't understand anything else after that because her speech was slurred with booze. She was three feet away from me, and she had the air reeking of alcohol.

"And another thing. I will whoop yo' white ass!" She bent down, picked up a Hennessey bottle, and began to chug.

"Maybe you should slow down." I put my hand on her arm, and she removed the bottle from her lips and looked at my hand as if it were a spider.

"Bitch! Get ya light, bright hands off me!" She screwed the top back on her drink. "Okay, Marjorie. It's about to go down." She bent over to set the drink down, and the weight of her body went with the bottle until she was in the grass.

I just stared. So sad. I didn't know what to do. If somebody found her, she would get kicked out of school for sure. I picked up her alcohol, gin and juice, Everclear, Hennessey, vodka, tequila, small shot bottles, and bottle of cranberry juice, and I threw them in the backseat. I picked up her light body and put her on the passenger side. I decided to leave the lawn chair.

I took her back to my place and told my friend something had come up and that I needed her to come to me instead. She got there twenty minutes later, and her heckling started as soon as the door was cracked.

"You never want to come see me; I always have to come see you. What? You too good to come to a dorm now?"

"Shhh!"

"No! Don't shhh me. I'm tired of making that walk, Kat."

I pointed to the couch.

"What are you pointing at? Ooooh, my God! Are you harboring colored fugitives?"

"Marley, what are you talking about?"

"Well…why is she here?"

"She passed out trying to fight me." I covered her with a blanket, wondering why I hadn't done so sooner.

"And you thought it was smart to bring her here? What if she wakes up and tries to kill you?"

I didn't know what Marley thought of black people, but I had a feeling it wasn't how I felt about them. I could tell her true feelings were certainly going to come out that night. "Marley, you're being ridiculous."

"Is she on drugs?" Before I could answer, she said, "She stinks of booze." She was in her face as if the girl was the missing link, and she had a front row seat to the show. "Was her kid with her?"

I just looked at her. This was getting better and better.

"Well, you know they all breed babies."

Breed?

She looked back at the girl. "Poor girl probably doesn't even know who the father is."

"Marley, get away from her. I invited you here to help me take care of her."

Without moving, she said, "Take care of her?"

Just then, the thin girl started rocking from side to side on the couch.

"I told you she was on drugs!" Marley didn't move and stared in amazement. Her mouth dropped as if she expected something big to happen.

And it did. The girl threw up all over Marley's face and green patent leather boots. I laughed so hard that I had to rush to the bathroom. When I came back into the living room, Marley had finished screaming and was in the kitchen running water all over her face and hair.

When all the vomit was gone and she was drenched from the top of her head to her shoulders, she shrieked, "It's not funny!"

For some reason, that made me laugh more.

"I don't know what's gotten into you, Kathryn Heine, but I won't let you influence me, and I will not help you take care of some nigger bitch!" She stomped out of the house, slamming the door behind her.

I called her a few weeks later.

"Hey, Marley."

"I don't know who this is. Is this the girl with the black friend?"

I just hung up. Marley and I never spoke again after that day. The day after I "rescued" her, my houseguest did not wake up till two in the afternoon to use the bathroom.

19

She had straight hair that bent at the ends and stopped at her shoulders. She walked straight past me to the bathroom as if she wasn't in a foreign place, still naked. I heard her come out of the bathroom, but I didn't see her. After five minutes, I left my homework and went looking for her. And there she was, in my bed, holding my teddy bear, snoring as loud as ever. I smiled, shut the door, and went back to my homework. The girl woke up two more times to pee and then one last time at 9:30 p.m.

"Um…"

I looked up, and she was standing there, hands on her hips, with an angry and confused look on her face.

"Hello."

"Hello? Why am I here? And why am I naked?"

As I told her what happened the night before, her face slowly softened.

"You tried to attack me, but you passed out before you could," I explained.

She crossed her arms and legs and looked away, and, under her breath, she mumbled, "Sorry."

"You're fine. I would have put some clothes on you, but…I don't know."

"That's fine. You got me out of the cold. That's more than anyone else would have done." Then, she looked me in my eyes and said, "Thank you. Hey. I'm Charlotte." She stuck her hand out. "What's your name?"

I shook it, laughed, and stood up. "Well, according to you, it's Sarah, Matilda, and, um, what was the last one? Marjorie!"

She smiled sheepishly.

"But my name is Kathryn, Kathryn Heine. But let's see if you can fit any of my clothes."

After that night, I went from being her protector to being her best friend. We developed a system. She carried a card in her bra with my name, address, and number on it. And, when things got kind of crazy at a party, she would have someone call me or drop her off at my house.

I think the last straw was when Charlotte got alcohol poisoning and was rushed to the hospital. As always, when I showed up, everyone was shocked to see a white girl coming to see a black girl. When I went in her room and saw her looking so pathetic, I made her promise to move in with me and stop drinking.

"I'll never take another drink," she said that day.

But the day when she moved in, my boyfriend brought over a case of beer to celebrate, and, before we finished our one, she had knocked back six beers. And that was when José started calling her Fish.

While living with Charlotte, I noticed that it took plenty of bottles of anything before she got drunk. She woke up drinking Bailey's without coffee. She drank vodka like it was Sprite, and she'd go to bed nowhere near drunk. Sometimes, she might have had a small buzz, but she was functioning, and, soon, I didn't know the difference between a drunk Fish and a sober Fish.

Fish was the greatest friend anybody could wish for, and all the guys wanted her. She used that to her advantage. I never asked her to pay for anything because I was handling it before I insisted that she move in. But she was very beautiful, and it got to the point where all she had to do was look sad and guys would give her money. Then, she would go out and buy groceries or pay a bill.

One unforgettable day was when José and I had broken up. She rushed into the house and laid across the foot of my bed with a goofy smile on her face.

21

"What?" I asked.

"Hello, friend."

"No!"

"No, what?"

"I don't know what you're going to ask for, but no." I went back to balancing my checkbook.

"Kitty Kat!" I looked up at Fish's mini- afro. I remember when she had the bright idea to go natural. It actually looked good on her.

"What, Charlotte?" I stopped what I was doing to look at her.

"Okay, I met a guy who wants to pay your rent for this month."

This can't be good, I thought, but I asked, "Where did you meet him?"

"At the ABC store."

"Jesus, Fish!"

"Just hear me out…"

"Let me guess. He wants to have a threesome?"

She just smiled.

"Really? Really?" I got up to go to the kitchen.

She followed, pleading, "Come on, Kat. Let's have some fun tonight."

"Tonight?" I looked her dead in the eye. "You already told him yes, didn't you?"

"Sort of."

"Sort of? Fish, you better start talking."

"Well, I figured you wouldn't turn down an extra few hundred dollars."

We argued for an hour, and then José called.

"Look, I just left your stuff outside your door," he said.

I ran to my front door and opened it, and there was the box of my stuff.

"Why didn't you just knock, so I could get it?" I asked, but he just hung up. I looked at Fish and said, "I'll do it."

She smiled from ear to ear. I don't know why that pissed me off, but it did.

That night, Mystery Man knocked on the door, and Fish let him in. He came in and sat on the loveseat, and the two of us sat on the couch.

He and Fish talked for a bit. Then, he said, "You guys ready? Your friend looks nervous."

It was true. I was, but Fish said, "Yeah, we're ready."

In one swift motion, Mystery Man pulled out his dick and started jerking off.

"Kiss her," he commanded.

Fish grabbed the back of my head, turned me toward her, and kissed me, forcing her tongue into my mouth. I was so scared that I didn't resist a bit, but I aggressively kissed her back as I stared at the man's penis from the corner of my eye. Finally closing my eyes, I lost myself in her kiss. The man continued to jack off as he watched us kissing. He watched Fish get me as worked up as she was.

Finally, the man stepped closer to us. He slowly leaned forward on the balls of his feet, and then slowly slid his dick in between our mouths. My eyes popped open, but Fish's didn't. I looked at her, then up at him. They were both so into it that I went right back in. We continued to kiss and lick each other's lips as he gently rocked his hips and slid his cock in and out of our kiss. He finally left it there a bit longer, and Fish took over. She licked the sides of his shaft in long strokes as she blew him. I backed away and watched as Fish formed a tight ring with her lips and slid it up and down his shaft.

"Fuck," I whispered.

He pulled back and started jerking off again, and Fish went back to kissing me. He watched us kiss for a few more minutes. Then, he watched as Fish slowly raised her hand and placed it over one of my breasts. She lightly rubbed on it, and I moaned softly into her mouth. My nipple rose to her touch, and she found it with her fingertips and gave it a gentle tug. He stepped toward me and rubbed his cock against my cheek.

Instinctively, like a baby when she feels her mother's nipple, I turned my head and wrapped my lips around his cock. I drew him deeper into my mouth, and I knew my guard had dropped. I lifted his big penis up and lapped at his testicles like a hungry dog. I sucked and licked with my tongue, and, with my hand, I stroked. Then, I spat on his dick and beat it with my hand. He moaned, and I knew that was my cue. I shoved him deep down in my mouth until he was playing patty cake with my tonsils. I gagged the first time, but, the next few times, I relaxed my throat and sucked him so deeply that my top lip was right above his pubic hair. My bottom lip quivered on his balls.

Fish looked up at me and bit her lips as she raised her other hand to my breasts. She deeply massaged them through my robe. Then, she took the robe off of me and undid my bra as I sucked him with long, deep strokes. My mouth was warm and wet, and I moved it very slowly and gently.

Fish dropped down to her knees beside me and reached for the elastic waistband of my thong. She, then, slipped her fingers under the elastic and gently eased them down. I never broke my rhythm on his cock as I pressed my feet against the floor and raised my ass off of the couch just enough for Fish to pull off my thong.

Once my thong was off and thrown across the room, I sat back down and spread my legs. Fish knelt down by my feet and placed her hands on my thighs as she leaned in and pressed her tongue against my clitoris. I moaned onto the man's cock as a bolt of pure erotica shot through my body. Fish pressed her face harder into my dripping wet pussy as she licked me stupid. I felt her tongue lapping me in long strokes from my ass to my clit, and my body shivered with excitement. All at once, Mystery Man put his hand on the back of my head, and I put my hand on the back of Fish's. I caught her stealing glances of me sucking his penis, and I knew she was being turned on.

Finally, Fish pulled away from my pussy and looked up at us. She sat down next to me on the couch and gave my pussy a few last rubs with her fingers before she said, "I want to watch him fuck you."

He took a step back, leaned down, and kissed me hard. He reached up and massaged my breasts as Fish took off her dress. She was completely naked underneath. Mystery Man laid me down on the couch, and Fish sat on the floor and spread her legs, watching as the man guided his cock into me.

"Fuck that pussy," Fish groaned.

Then, she licked two of her fingers and slipped them into her pussy while she watched me being fucked.

I moaned loader and loader as the man followed Fish's commands.

"Fuck her. Fuck her harder," she said as she rolled her nipples between her fingers and pulled on them violently. "Bury that cock in her tight, little pussy."

He was pounding me furiously, and I was loving it. I moaned so loud that I was afraid the neighbors might hear us. My face tightened up as my breasts bounced with each thrust. I looked over at Fish and found her rubbing her clit faster than ever. Her face twisted in knots as she occasionally slipped two or three fingers deep inside of herself before pulling them out and licking them.

"Yeah! Yeah! Oh, fuck that pussy!" she shouted.

Mystery Man rolled on the floor, pulling me with him, so I was now on top. He turned me around, so I was forced to look at Fish in the backwards cowgirl position. As I got into it, I rode him vigorously, and we both watched Fish as she rubbed her pussy faster and faster. The man reached up, wrapped his arms around me, and squeezed my nipples as I bounced on his cock. That totally did the job for Fish, and we watched as her body shook and white fluid squirted from between her fingers and dripped down her asshole.

I had found my rhythm by then, and I was getting close to coming, too. He flexed his hips upwards and pushed his cock forward as far as he could and quickly found my G-spot. I screamed and let my hot liquid gush out and surround his massive penis. I didn't stop. I couldn't stop. He felt so good inside, even better than before now that my pussy muscles were tight on him.

"I'm coming!" he shouted. He threw me off of him, stood up, and used my juices as lubricant to jerk off.

Fish crawled over to him and sat at his feet like an eager puppy. I stood next to him and used my hand to bring him to a raging orgasm.

"Fuck! Fuck!" he yelled as the contents of his happy ending shot all over Fish's face and into her waiting mouth.

Once he was done, Fish opened her eyes and closed her mouth, and we heard her swallow his saltiness. She, then, picked up her dress and wiped off her face before standing up and kissing me. Mystery Man dressed, handed me six hundred dollars, and said, "You guys rock!"

26

We never knew his name.

I washed my hands and my dildo. That story always got me hot in the pants. I combed my hair, threw a nightgown on, and went back to my office.

Boy Toy

For my own personal reasons, I would like to remain anonymous. I have agreed to tell all my secrets, but, as of now, I am not comfortable revealing my identity.

I guess I should tell you a little about myself, right? Okay, well, I'm a twenty-one-year-old man, and I am a college student, studying fashion design. I want to start my own clothing line for plus-sized girls. I am five foot nine, Latino and Caucasian, I have brown hair, and…I'm gay.

I think I first knew I was officially gay in the ninth grade. In middle school, I was feminine, and everyone thought I was, but I kept denying it. For years, I lied to myself. I've had, probably, five real girlfriends. All of them were madly in love with me, but I never was in love with them. In fact, I remember the day I knew I was gay, and that same day was the day I had my first gay sexual experience.

I had seen the fliers around school for football tryouts, and I decided to go, hoping it would make my dad proud and put some hair on my chest. I got there, and, to my surprise, I was smaller than the older boys…much smaller. Every one of them was pushing six feet or taller, and they all looked like they spent way too much time in the gym. And then, there was Martin Luke, the guy with two first names. He was over six feet tall, caramel-skinned, and he had brown dreads that tapped his shoulders. He was the god of the football team, basketball team, wrestling team...all the teams. Every muscle on him bulged without him flexing.

On that particular day, we were all in the locker room. The room smelled of nothing but stench and sweat...and we hadn't even started working out yet. There were four aisles surrounded by lockers. The room looked as if a big blue monster had thrown up blue juice all over the place. The floor was gray with blue specks. The lockers were blue. The walls were painted dark blue and light blue, and the showers had blue tile on the floor. It was enough to make my brain hurt.

Well, Martin was wearing nothing but a cup and some old tennis shoes. He was talking to a friend and leaning up against the blue lockers.

"Whoa! Looks like we got a faggot trying out for the team!" Chris Maddox sneered.

I looked down, and my seven-inch dick was so erect that I could've hung everyone's coats on it. I didn't know what to say. I looked up at Martin.

"See something you like, faggot?"

I couldn't speak.

"Hold him down."

Every guy in the locker room came toward me. I pushed through them all and ran out on the field. Why was I still trying out? I wondered. All of the boys came outside with Martin Luke front and center. I turned away for fear of making eye contact, and, out of my peripheral vision, I saw something huge coming straight toward me. I turned right into Martin Luke's fist as it smashed into my cheek, and I fell to the ground.

"Don't you ever look at me again, faggot!"

"What's going on?" Jamar Jackson, a senior football player, yelled as he ran up to the huddle.

"This faggot was checking us out!" Chris yelled.

"So you beat him up?" Jamar asked as he helped me up. "You know what, Martin? You're only beating up on him because he's smaller than you. How 'bout you fight me?" Jamar, who towered over Martin, said. Then, he waited for a response.

"Man, fuck you!" Martin yelled.

As he turned to walk away, Jamar grabbed Martin by his shoulder, spun him around, and socked him in the face. Martin Luke dropped to the ground, and all of the boys started yelling and laughing.

Coach came running up to the huddle and asked, "What the hell is going on?"

About fifty boys started yelling, trying to explain what had happened, and the only words I heard were "this faggot."

"Hey! Hey! Hey!" Coach yelled. "One person at a time." He looked at Jamar. "Tell me what happened."

"When I came out here, Martin and his friends were trying to beat up this guy for being gay."

Coach was obviously mad as he looked at each of us. "So I guess you met the captain of the football team…Jamar Jackson. Jamar here is a great leader—not because I trained him, and not because he can knock a man out in one punch—" We all looked at Martin Luke, who was still on the ground, motionless. "But because he does what's right! He has integrity! He is respectful! He is loyal! And, for the few of you who will make my team, you will learn these same qualities." He glared at us all. "Understood?"

"Yes," some boys mumbled.

Jamar stepped forward. "When addressing an elder or anyone in authority, you address them as 'sir' or 'ma'am'! Understood?"

"Yes, sir!" we all shouted.

"Good," Coach said. "Everybody, except this young man, will stay back, run the field, and put up the equipment." He pointed to me, and moans and groans rang out over the crowd of boys. "You should have thought about that before you started picking on somebody smaller than you!"

We carried on with the tryouts, and, when we were done, the coach ordered pizza for himself and me. We sat in his office while we watched the guys run. After all that had happened, I couldn't stop gazing at those boys as they ran with their shirts off, muscles bulging, dreads bouncing, cornrows dangling, hair blowing, and—

"So you really are gay?"

I looked over at the coach, and he pointed to my now-hard cock. I covered it immediately. What is wrong with me? Why can't I control it? I wondered.

"Don't worry. Your secret's safe with me, but you're going to have to do a way better job of hiding it."

I put my head down in embarrassment.

The guys left in time to catch the activity bus. I didn't want to ride with them, so I pretended to lose track of time while cleaning the locker room. When he was ready to leave, Coach came out of his office, and he was shocked to see me.

"What are you doing here, kid?"

"I was cleaning up and lost track of time."

"You sure as hell did. Do you know what time it is?"

I looked at my cell phone. "Ten o'clock."

"Damn right! Now, how are you getting home? Do your parents know you're here?"

"My parents are out of town, so I was going to walk."

He paused for a moment. Then, he set his stuff down. "Look, I'll take you home." He hesitated. "But you got to do something for me."

As he walked toward me, I backed up. I kept backing up until I was against the wall. Coach Krisby grabbed my shoulders and turned me around. He pinned me up against the wall while he yanked my shorts and boxers down.

"Now, you be a good faggot."

I felt him struggling to pull his pants down. He let me go, so he could pull them down with ease, and I tried to run.

He grabbed me. "Where you going, boy? You know you want it!" He forced me onto my knees, yanked my head back, and said, "If you bite it, I'll kill you." Then, he forced his massive dick into my mouth and face fucked me.

I gagged. Then, I threw up the contents of my pepperoni dinner. It splattered on the locker room floor. I had never sucked a dick before.

"Get up," he said. When I did, he pointed to the bench. "Lay down."

I did, and then it happened. He slowly put the head of his cock in my virgin asshole. I was scared, but I wanted him to. I mean, I really just wanted to know what it would feel like. As he slowly moved the head in and out, I relaxed.

"You like that, faggot?"

I nodded. I did. Then, I didn't. As he kept going deeper and deeper, the pain became so horrid that I wanted to cry. I almost did, but I couldn't let him see me cry. He enjoyed it. He moaned and moaned, and hearing him moan turned me on. I motioned for him to let me get up. When he did, I put one knee on the bench and put my other foot on the ground. With my ass in the air, I grabbed my cock and started stroking it. He liked that.

"Oh, yeah! Beat that dick."

I beat it harder and harder as he rammed me harder and harder. He smacked my ass with his right hand and put his left one under my shirt and played with my nipples. I could hear him about to cum, and it made me want to explode. I beat my dick faster, and he fucked me harder until I was coming and shooting it all the way across the locker room. He pulled out, turned me around, and beat his dick until my face was covered in his goo. I never stopped jacking off, and seeing him explode with pleasure made me cum again. I laid back on the bench as my body vibrated and cum erupted out of me like lava out of a volcano. Coach was still coming, and it landed on my stomach.

I laid there, shaking with passion. When I finally stopped, I licked the cum off my fingers. I wiped the cum off my stomach and face and licked my fingers clean. Coach was about to get a towel to wipe his dick off, but I grabbed him, shoved his massiveness in my mouth, and sucked the cum off of it, too. I looked up to see if he liked it, and his face was blank. I stopped.

"Put your clothes on. Let's go."

What? I was confused. I tried to look in his face for an answer, but he didn't look my way. He just got dressed, got his things, and said, "I'll be waiting in the truck."

The ride home was long, and, right before I got out the truck, he said, "Nothing happened tonight."

My face was full of shock. I got out the truck, and the bastard didn't even wait to see if I got in safely before he sped off.

Later that night, I couldn't sleep, trying to figure out what happened. The more I thought about what happened, the harder and hornier I got. Before I knew it, I was humping my fist and gripping my bed. I imagined Coach spraying my face with white semen, and I had an orgasm all over again. I didn't clean myself up. It was so good; my hand was still gripping my dick when I fell asleep. I woke up at three a.m. beating my dick. I must've started in my sleep because I didn't remember beginning; I just remembered being about to cum. Three more times that night, I woke up jacking off to the memory of me and Coach Krisby. The next morning, as I put my sheets in the wash, I thought, There's no denying it now. I'm gay. I smiled as I thought, And I like it.

Jen

It'd been nearly a month since I'd broken up with the Whore. That was the name I'd given Tony, my ex. I found out he had cheated on me several times with several different girls, so, in my mind, he was the Whore. But I couldn't deny I was in love with the bastard, and dealing with the breakup had been hard as hell! In a month, I'd gone from a size fourteen to a sixteen!

My mom's friend, Charlotte, offered to take me to the gym with her. Charlotte was a few years younger than Mom with a personality to match! She was forty-six, looked twenty-five, acted eighteen...perfect! I was twenty-three, looked twenty-three, and I acted eighteen.

She had been a freshman when my mom was a senior in college. They were best friends then, and, now, many years later, we were best friends. Charlotte had never had kids, so, when my brother Mike and I were younger, she bought the stuff our parents wish they could've bought us. Back then, she had been Aunty; now she was Sis. Mike once made the mistake of calling her Aunty in public when he was sixteen. We thought Charlotte was going to have a heart attack.

"Michael! You can't go around calling me your aunt in public! That's just as bad as calling me Granny! From now on, I'm your sister!"

Sis and I went to the gym twice a week. She had such a banging body that I felt diminished standing next to her. She and I were almost the same height, about five foot three inches. She was slim with a tiny butt, and her breasts were a little bigger than mine. I was a D, and I think she was a DD. But even though next to her I felt like the seven hundred pound man, I loved being around her.

After a couple of weeks of working out with her, I had lost the weight I had gained, but I still wasn't happy with my appearance. In the locker room, she would shower in the group showers, and I would shower in the stalls. Sometimes, she would tease me for going in and taking my clothes with me.

"Oooooh, are you hiding a wee wee in your pants, Jen? Are you really a boy?"

I would throw a towel at her, and we would laugh about it. Once or twice I would catch a glimpse of Charlotte as she dropped her towel and her back was to me. A lot of women got dressed and undressed in front of us without a second thought, and there were some pretty gross sights, but Sis...she was different. I didn't look at her in admiration; it was more like envy. The first thing I noticed was her brown skin. I always thought African-Americans and Latinos were special, but, even being half-Latino, I didn't feel as special next to Charlotte.

I would like to stop here and say that I have never had a sexual thought about women, only the normal random curiosities. However, something happened; a change began.

A simple conversation sparked my curiosity. It started out as nothing. I just asked, "Sis, how come you don't have a boyfriend?"

She laughed and said, "Jen, I'm a lesbian!"

I didn't know what to say. In fact, I was embarrassed at my stumbling response. "Oh, uh… um… oh…wow… okay."

Sis laughed out loud. I don't know why I was shocked. I guess I was shocked at the fact that someone I'd known for so long had this secret, and she was not what I expected or assumed her to be. The way she told me was so casual; it was like it wasn't something she wanted to be a secret. She asked me in a very concerned tone if I was cool with it, and, when I found my voice, I replied, "Yeah. Why wouldn't I be cool with you being a dike? No! No, no, no! I mean…uh…wait…Why wouldn't I be cool with you being a lesbo? Noooo, that wasn't right. Um…Yeah, Sis, I'm cool with it."

She laughed and kissed me on the forehead. She had kissed me before, but, this time, I got a tingle down my spine. I don't know why; it wasn't like she had kissed me on the lips or anything. I tried not to let it dwell on my mind, but, when I went to bed that night, I started thinking about the friends she had introduced my family and me to over the years. Were they really just friends? Or were they girlfriends?

When I closed my eyes, I started thinking about how she must have been with them in bed. I imagined her sweaty brown body against their light, white bodies, or even the caramel-colored ones. I imagined her shaking as each one of her "friends" gave her an orgasm. I imagined the faces she'd made as they licked her clit and ran their fingers through her afro. Before too long, I found I was rubbing myself at the thought and tasting my own juices from my fingers. I only brought myself back to reality when I moaned as my tongue tasted my pussy juices.

What the hell was I thinking? I hadn't had those thoughts since I had first really tasted myself with Tony. I dismissed it as just being overly horny from missing him still, and I went off to sleep.

The next time I went to the gym, I knew my thoughts about Sis had changed. Every time I looked at her, I couldn't help thinking about her with her friends over the years and what they had been up to in the bedroom. I even started to watch lesbian porn at home and look for pictures and movies with small black-haired women that looked like Sis. It got worse when, after two or three weeks, I stopped picturing her with friends and started picturing her with me.

Every time she touched me, I felt tingles go through my body, and my heart fluttered whenever she walked in the room. Eventually, I stopped kidding myself, and, at night, I imagined her kissing me and stroking me as I rubbed myself to orgasm. It was her hands that took me there, even her tongue made me cum. I knew this wasn't good. It would only end in heartbreak. I would gain weight again and spend my nights in tears, instead of orgasms.

It took me weeks of wrinkled fingertips and messed up sheets before I couldn't take it anymore. I had to see Sis naked. But when I went to the showers and the thought of my body standing among a group of perfect bodies…I couldn't. Then, one day, I had no choice. As I turned the corner to go into the stall, a big red sign with white letters blocked the entrance: OUT OF ORDER.

Oh, shit! Oh, shit! Oh, shit! I kept saying to myself. My heart was beating at a million miles per hour, and I began to feel sick, embarrassed, and excited all at once. We had just come from the pool, so I still had my one piece on as I walked up to Sis, who was already soaping up with her back to me. Feeling very uncomfortable about stripping, I quickly undressed and took the shower next to hers. She was clearly shocked to see me standing there.

"My shower is broken, so I had no choice but to—"

"It's okay. You're allowed in here, too!" She laughed.

That humor relaxed me a little, and, as I soaped up, I stole glances of her body. Even then, as my hands rubbed past my nipples, I wished it was her experienced hands washing me and not my lonely ones. I'd never wanted somebody to touch me so badly. I felt as if my whole body was going to go into a shaking frenzy from craving attention—her attention. Her breasts looked beautiful, slightly bigger than mine with small, dark nipples. I tried to keep my glances short and natural as I watched the soap drip down her smooth, brown stomach to her shaven, wet, very small, protruding pussy lips. After all the porn I'd watched on my computer, I wanted to get on my knees and lick her right there.

As I washed my hair, I thought I could get a better sneak peek of her body, but I got another surprise, instead. Charlotte obviously thought my eyes were closed because she was licking her lips and checking me out! She had even moved her head down to get a closer look at my pussy. As I rinsed my hair, I noticed she had her back to me again, and I couldn't help but wonder if she actually wanted me. Me? No! But wasn't she looking?

We dried off and went to our lockers to get dressed. Normally, Sis would have had her back to me while we clothed ourselves, but, this time, she faced me. Even though I tried to look her in the eyes, I couldn't help but take quick glances at her breasts and her pussy, and she was even touching my arm a little more than usual. As I bent over to pull my skirt up, her butt touched mine, and I nearly climaxed right there!

"Uh, Sis, I'll meet you in the café. I have to go to the restroom right quick."

"Okay." She grabbed her things, and I raced for the restroom.

As soon as I sat on the toilet, I let my fingers slip between my slit to my already hard clit and massaged out my fantasies. I tried, but I couldn't stop moaning. I even covered my mouth when I heard someone come in, but even that didn't help, and I took myself on a roller coaster ride. Finally, I had an orgasm, cleaned myself up, redressed, and stepped out to wash my hands.

The other stall opened, and Sis stepped out. "You okay, sweetie?"

"Oh, uh, yeah. I think I ate something bad last night. That's why you might've heard...well. "

She smiled. "Let's go."

We ate at the café, and she took me home. All of a sudden, I felt that I had messed up.

Fuck!

CHARLOTTE

What the fuck is wrong with me? I am forty-six years old. Why am I fantasizing about a twenty-three-year-old kid?

It was two a.m., and I was putting my sheets in the wash. I could not stop masturbating since I had dropped Jen off at her house. I couldn't get her body out of my mind. In fact, I hadn't been able to get her out of my mind since we started going to the gym together. It was as if the more time I spent with her, the more attractive she became to me. At times, I caught myself trying to peek in her shower stall to catch glimpses of her. But, today, I actually saw her naked. She wasn't that little girl anymore. Those tan nipples, that long hair...I had always thought she was beautiful, but working out had made her body more toned. And our conversation at the café was...I don't know, but I surely blew my cover. I had asked if she had her eyes on any boys, and she turned it around and asked if I had my eyes on any girls. I blushed like a shy schoolgirl! I didn't even know black people could blush!

"Come on. Tell me," she said, laughing, showing that pretty, white, childlike smile.

"I can't."

"Well, you asked me about guys! I can't ask you about girls? At least, tell me about her."

I threw my hands up. "Okay! Okay! She is a lovely, sweet girl, a bit younger than me, really smart, really pretty, but I don't think she would be interested in me."

"Why do you think that? Isn't she gay? It's not like you're ugly or anything."

"No, she's not gay. And I don't want to approach her because I would hate to lose her as a friend."

She put her hand on my arm and tried to sound as mature as possible when she said, "Well, wasn't it you that told me 'there are times when you have to go with your heart and not your head'?"

It was true. I had said that, but, this was a sticky situation. I quickly changed the subject, and the topic was never brought up again. When I dropped her off at her house, I pecked her on the cheek as usual and watched her until she got in the house safely.

When I got home that night, I didn't know what to do. Had I hinted too much that I was an old perv? Well, I wasn't a perv because she was twenty-three. But still, I'd known her since birth! I decided to get online and do some work. I ran an online clothing store that was so prosperous that I was able to afford a big five-bedroom house that I didn't need. I lived there alone: no husband, no wife, and no children. I didn't even buy the house with the intent of having any of the above; I bought it just because I could afford it. I was looking at some cute lingerie when I got an IM…from Jen! I opened it.

Jen: Hey, Sis
Charlotte: Hey, babe

The fact that I thought about her like that and she called me Sis made me sick to my stomach.

Charlotte: What'chu doin' up this late… or early?
Jen: Nothing just sitting here thinking about what we talked about earlier. It's sad you feel you can't ask that girl out.
Charlotte: I didn't say I can't; I said I am scared to.
Jen: Well, is she a good friend?
Charlotte: Yes
Jen: Does she know you're gay?
Charlotte: Yes
Jen: So a good friend should take it as a compliment, shouldn't she?
Charlotte: Ha! Ha! I wish it was that easy!
Jen: But why is it hard? I would take it as a compliment.

Whoa! Was she…did she know it was her? Maybe, I should fish for info.

Charlotte: Really? Even if you weren't gay or bi?
Jen: Well, maybe some people keep it a secret better. LOL
Charlotte: Maybe they do. LOL. Listen, babe. I got to go. Getting tired. I'll hit u up tomorrow. Hugs - xxxxx
Jen: G'nite and you're welcome - xxxxx

When I hit that little red x in the top right corner, I couldn't believe how much I couldn't wait for Monday, so I could see her at the gym again. As I returned to my lingerie shopping, I got an idea.

Charlotte: What are you doing tomorrow?
Jen: Nothing, watching the Adventure Time marathon. Y, whaddup?
Charlotte: Well, I got some gift cards and wanted to know if you wanted to go shopping with me
Jen: You need fashion advice, too? :)
Charlotte: Yeah. You know I'm helpless without you! LOL
Jen: Hmmm… food? Yes, no, maybe?
Charlotte: Yes, Fatty McFat! LOL, jk. It's a deal.
Jen: A deal or a date? LOL

Oh, shit! What do I say?

Charlotte: Both for you, gorgeous LOL

Swag…are we flirting?

Jen: Well, you know me, anything 4 food. Do I get to try stuff on 2?

Charlotte: If ur good, I might even buy you something. :)
Jen: Yay! See u tomorrow - xxxxxxxx
Charlotte: Byyyye! xxxxx

This should be fun!

The next morning, I put on my white lace panties, no bra, and a brown low-cut sundress. The sundress had a split on both sides that crept up my thighs almost to my waist. The dress was halter style and tied behind my neck, showing off my arms and my back. I put on my gold watch, three gold bracelets, and my gold sandals. I sprayed my 'fro, ran my hands through it, got my keys, and left.

When I pulled up, Jen was sitting outside. As she walked to the car, I saw she was wearing a navy blue cotton skirt with white horizontal stripes, and the hemline stopped right beneath her butt. She had on a V-neck white tee and a cut-off denim jacket, and she clearly wasn't wearing a bra either (the jacket must be so Kathryn wouldn't see her without a bra on).

"Wow! You look great, Jen!"

She blushed a little. "You look pretty hot yourself, Sis."

There went that name again. She got into the passenger seat and leaned over to kiss me on the cheek as usual, but, at the last second, I turned my head, and her kiss landed on my lips. It was only a quick second kiss, but her lips felt soft against mine, and, as I pulled back, she looked shyly out of the window. Oh, no! I thought. We said nothing as we set off for the mall.

It was Saturday, and Lynnhaven Mall was busy with women doing shopping stress relief while toting around their demon spawn. It seemed as if every kid was drooling either from their mouths or their noses. When we passed a toy store, there was nothing but little children screaming for things they wanted that their parents had no intentions of buying. I was disgusted. Why, as a parent, would you even set yourself up for the embarrassment? If you didn't have a plan to buy a toy, why go in the store? And why don't parents beat their kids anymore? Had I screamed because my mother wouldn't buy me something, she surely would have smacked me twice and set me straight. Hmm. I didn't have kids for a reason.

We window-shopped a little, and then I dragged her into Lu Lu's Boutique. Lu Lu's was a really nice, locally-owned lingerie boutique, one of my favorite stores.

The lady who owned it had candles burning, and, every time I inhaled, I took a deep breath of something wonderful. That day, it was pumpkin spice. The walls were painted orange and pink, and there was a glass table with a five foot tall orchid centerpiece placed carefully in the middle. Sprinkled on the table were decorative crystals, and wrapped around the table was a circular orange ottoman. It was in the center of the store, and it had pink pillows on it. Lu Lu had, also, baked miniature cookies that she kept in the back of the store between the edible underwear, alcoholic whipped cream, and edible body butter.

I picked out six pieces of different types of lingerie and dragged Jen into the fitting room with me. As soon as I had drawn the curtain, I pulled the sundress up over my head, revealing my lace panties. I saw Jen trying not to stare, but it was hard for her. Good! I thought.

I tried on piece after piece of lingerie, bending over dramatically when I had to take off something or put something on.

"Are you going to wear one of those for your lady friend?"

I giggled. Of course, baby! I wanted to say, but I didn't answer.

"Which one do you think I should get?"

"Well, the one with the breasts cut out is tacky. The green one, that's nothing but lace, so that's awesome. And the leopard trimmed in red really looks good against your skin."

"Well, I'll get those two, since you like them so much."

"Well, my opinion is not important, the mystery girl's is."

"Do you have any lingerie?"

"No." She laughed. "Boys get turned on whether you're covered up like a nun or not. Lingerie isn't needed."

"Wait here."

"What?"

I went out into the store and came back with four pieces of lingerie. "Try these on." I thrust the items at her.

"What?"

"Jen Marie Matos, if you say 'what' one more time, I will put a hurtin' on you." I gave her a look that showed I meant it.

She stood up, stripped down to her pink thong, and looked at me as if she had never done that before. I helped her into the different pieces of underwear. We laughed as she made funny poses. I took my phone out and took some pictures, and she laughed. Then, she put on a black one. It was all black except for a tiny red bow between her breasts and below her navel. The top was like a tank top, but the midriff was cut open to show her smooth stomach. It stopped at her waist to show her black lace thong.

"You look amazing in that one."

She turned and looked in the mirror, and, at the sight of that perfect ass, I crept up behind her, put my arms around her, and pulled her in closer to me. We looked at each other in the mirror.

She turned to face me. "Am I the girl?"

I kissed her, slightly longer than when we were in the car, but still merely a peck. And then, looking deep into her beautiful gray eyes, I said, "Of course, it's you!"

Then, we kissed properly.

As I felt her young, tender lips against mine, something came over me. I felt young and wild. She let my tongue inside her mouth to enjoy the party. I caressed her back, keeping her body close against mine, and then moved my hands down to her bottom. I indulged in her kiss; I quickly forgot where we were. All I wanted was her, to touch her, to kiss her, and I didn't want to stop when I did.

"Let's go to my place."

She didn't say anything, just kept breathing heavily. "You need some help getting dressed?"

She nodded. I undid the clasps that were holding the teddy together, and, at the sight of her free breasts, I was turned on even more. She moaned loudly as I sucked on her nipples. I pulled her thong down with my teeth, and she whispered frantically, "No, no, no!" I licked her pussy lips with one sweep of my tongue and then hurriedly got her dressed.

When we stepped out of the dressing room, the owner looked at us. She had heard.

"Problem?" I asked.

She gave me a disgusted look. I took a handful of cookies and threw a look back at her as I said, "Let's go, Jen."

In the car, I could tell she was still in a daze, but I put her face in my hands and kissed her deeply. As I pulled away, I said, "I have wanted this for so long! You have no idea." I started the car and drove as fast as I could to my house.

As we walked into the house, Jen turned around, looked me in my eyes, and said, "I've never done anything like this with a girl before, but I'm so happy it was me you wanted."

I smiled. "I want you more than you can ever imagine. Come on."

I stuck out my hand and led her to my bedroom. The room was a decent size with a king-sized bed in the middle and two nightstands on either side of it. Atop the nightstands were two table lamps and inside the nightstands were my "little helpers"—things I used, from time to time, that helped me with my orgasms. There was a vanity dresser on the far wall and a bathroom to the right of the bedroom door. I undressed her and then myself.

"Do you trust me?" I could see the nervousness on her face.

"Um, sure."

"Good." I took a towel from the bathroom and laid it on the king-sized bed, "Lie down and close your eyes." She gave me a confused and scared look. "Trust me."

She laid down. I went down the hall and came back a few moments later. When she heard me come back in the room, she lifted her head.

"I can see you like to peek. I'm going to have to fix that." I pulled out a blindfold from my nightstand and gently pulled it over her eyes. I stroked her soft pubic hair and turned on my surprise. She must have thought it was a vibrator because she opened her legs a little wider as if inviting pleasure to come. I couldn't help but laugh as I moved the object from the top of her pussy to her lips.

She gasped. "Oh, my God! Are you shaving me?"

We both burst out into laughter, and I couldn't go on; I was so weak. When I finally regained my composure, I turned the clippers back on and continued shaving. I had fantasized almost every day of tasting Jen with my tongue and smearing her juices all over my mouth, but in none of my fantasies did I enjoy a mouthful of hair! I separated her legs a little more, squirted shave gel on her, and gently caressed it into her skin. As I took the razor to her skin, I kept my thumb on her hard clit, playing with it and teasing it. The whole time I was shaving, Jen was moaning little, sweet moans, and, when I was satisfied with my masterpiece, I turned the clippers back on and rested them against her clit as I buried two fingers deep inside her hole. Her body lifted up automatically as she yelped with an incredible mix of tingles and sparks, and it was only seconds before she hit the orgasm I had worked so hard to build for her. She giggled; I smiled. I kissed on her chest and neck, slowly working my way up to her lips. She threw her arms around my neck and kissed me greedily. As we kissed, I put her hand on her own pussy.

"Feel for yourself."

She felt her smooth pussy and started to play with herself while I caressed her breasts and pinched her nipples. She started to move her hand.

"Keep going. You're turning me on."

She did. When I put her free hand on her breasts, she got the message. She played with her breasts with one hand and the one touching her sweet pussy moved faster and faster. I couldn't resist touching myself while I tried to imagine what she was thinking behind that blindfold.

I had an idea. I left her fighting her fingers for an orgasm. When I came back, I moved her hand and climbed on top of her. As I entered her dripping wet vagina, she yanked the blindfold off, and her face was full of fear. She hadn't expected me to be on the other end of that penis. The dildo hooked up to my harness was lifelike. It was nothing like the hard rubber ones that were sold in the stores. It was more natural and a whopping eight inches. As I started fucking her like a man, her shock disappeared. She pulled me to her, pinching my nipples as she kissed me, and my thrusting got faster. After a few minutes of violent thrusts, nipple sucking, and tongue kissing, we reached our orgasms together, and I only wished I could fill her pussy full of man cum.

To my surprise, when I pulled the big dick from inside her, she sat on her knees and licked her juices off the dildo. Then, she shoved all eight inches down her throat until her nose touched my stomach. Impressive.

"I used to practice on my toys when I was with Tony, and," she giggled, "I found out I don't have a gag reflex, so sucking dick is quite easy."

"Wow!" I laid down in the bed. "So, what do you think of your new, smooth look?"

She looked in the mirror, did a Superman pose, and smiled. I asked her again as she walked back over to the bed.

She kissed me and said, "I love it, but what's more important is that you take care of it like you did today."

I hugged her and said, "As long as you let me, baby. I've wanted you for so long; I'm never going to let you go."

"Well, I'm not going anywhere." She hugged me for a bit. Then, she unbuckled the strap on my harness and threw it on the floor.

What is this kid about to do? I wondered.

She straddled my body and began her kisses from the tip of my nose, across my lips, down my neck, down my tits, and she slowly moved down my belly.

"Oh, my God! You are about to make every dream I've ever had come true."

She just smiled and moved to my moist slit. Her kisses moved down my smooth skin, beside my small pussy lips. Between each kiss, she gave a little twirl of her tongue on my flesh, and, each time, her tongue moved closer to the most sensitive part of my body. My gasps and trembling increased until I yelled, "Please, just lick me, Jen! I'm begging you!"

She flicked her tongue from left to right across my swollen lips, each contact causing a jump from my body, and then she plunged her tongue deep into my hole. The top of her mouth covered the top of my lips and clitoris. I groaned with pleasure as she licked hard then soft and then added two fingers to my hole to add to the pleasure. I grabbed handfuls of her long hair, holding her head in place on my rock-hard clit. She nibbled on it, and I screamed, begging her to do it again. She did…many times! I nearly knocked the poor girl off the bed as I bucked like a pissed off donkey and my orgasm rippled through my entire body. She pushed her tongue deeper into me, as deep as she could reach, lapping up the large amounts of cum my tightening pussy was forcing out. She kept licking me until I begged her to stop because I couldn't take it anymore. I laid there, panting, and she crawled up the bed and kissed me. I smiled with my eyes closed.

"So, was that good for my first time?"

I opened my eyes. "It wasn't your first time!"

She smiled and nodded.

I laid my head back and closed my eyes. "Fucking…awesome."

She gently ran her fingers through my afro and then slowly traced her fingers over the skin of my shoulders and then down to my bullet-like nipples. I felt her get off the bed, and, when I opened my eyes, she had my strap-on on and was looking at herself, stroking the lifelike penis in the mirror. She jumped as I came behind her and kissed her neck. My hand came around and started to caress her breasts, and, in my other hand, I held a bottle of lotion, which I squirted on her new penis. She stroked it more as if she had been born with it. As I moved away from her, she turned to see me bent over my dresser. My eyes fixed on hers in the mirror, and a cute little smile appeared on my face.

She walked slowly over to me and ran her hand over my tiny, sexy ass, all the while stroking that penis. She teased both of my holes with it, finally resting it against my pussy. I closed my eyes as my pussy lips stretched to take the width of her tool as she slid it fully into me with one, slow movement. I moaned as it reached its full depth, and she pumped in and out. I knew this felt as good for her as it did for me because her moans were matching mine as the dresser shook with each lunge forward. I had my hand rubbing furiously on my own clit, and I knew that the part of the strap that was stimulating hers was doing its job. We truly came together. She slumped over me, and we both panted like thirsty dogs with our orgasms shaking our bodies. She slowly removed her thickness from me and cum dripped from my vagina and down the dresser. I helped her remove her maleness. We climbed under the sheets and drifted off into a very contented, very relaxed sleep.

Boy Toy

Coach Krisby and I had sex a few more times after that, each time ending the same as before, with me wanting more and him pretending that nothing happened. I thought it was our dirty, little secret, but, one night, after the football players had gone and the Coach had used me as a human masturbation piece, I was alone in the locker room, cleaning myself up.

"Hey."

I jumped and turned around. It was Jamar, standing there, looking at me with his arms crossed.

"What are you still doing here?" he asked.

"Uh, cleaning up."

He looked me up and down. "With your pants unbuttoned and your shirt halfway on?"

I looked myself over. "I don't like to get my clothes dirty, so when nobody's here, I—"

"Save it. I know what's going on."

I swallowed hard. "What are you talking about?"

"Don't worry. Your secret's safe with me." He sat on a locker room bench.

I laughed nervously. "I don't know what you're talking about."

"You and Coach Krisby."

My mouth went cotton dry, and I knew my skin went pale.

"It's okay. I'm not going to tell anybody." He looked me in my eyes. "But you should stop messing with him."

51

"Why?"

"Why? Because what do you get out of it? He's not your boyfriend, is he?"

"No."

"And does he buy you things or give you money?"

"No."

"So, he's not your sugar daddy either." He paused. "Do you get off when he fucks you?"

I hurriedly buttoned my shirt. "Yeah!" I didn't make eye contact.

"Hmm. Because he sucks your dick?"

I laughed nervously again. "No."

"Oh, because you fuck him?"

I moved the hair out of my eyes. "No."

Jamar just stared at me. "Because you jerk yourself off?"

I was hesitant for a moment. "Yeah."

Jamar stood up. "I'm no expert on gay relationships, but I've dated a few girls before, so I'm just assuming you guys are alike. It seems to me that you're his boy toy."

I looked up at him with a look of pure devastation. "No, he's not using me. It's just sex."

"To him, it's just sex. But not to you, and I can tell."

I didn't speak. I didn't know what to say.

"Hey! I'll give you a ride home."

After that night, I never talked to Jamar again. I saw him in passing, but that was it. I liked him as a person because he just came and gave me some advice. He genuinely wanted the best for me, but I had no idea why.

Eventually, I told Coach Krisby no more. I couldn't take being used for his pleasures. After I finished speaking, he looked me in my eyes and laughed. I felt pure humiliation, and I decided that it was best to try to forget about the past and press forward.

Not long after football tryouts, it had floated around school that I was a raging faggot. So, of course, it wasn't a surprise that I was joked about and bullied every day and moment, especially when Jamar wasn't around. It just became easier to isolate myself. I lost crazy amounts of weight because I skipped lunch. In high school, I sat in the very first seat of the bus. I was, also, the last stop, so, for forty-five seconds, it was just me and the bus driver, Mr. Earl.

Mr. Earl was always nice to me. He was an older, Caucasian man, about fifty or so, and he had brown hair with white and gray hairs that highlighted it. He wore a silver wedding band on his left hand, and he always wore brown loafers. For forty-five minutes, I had to endure teasing and random shit being thrown at me. But for the last few seconds of my ride, Mr. Earl would try to spark conversations and would even give me king-size candy bars or a variety of assorted snacks.

But things changed when, one day, I was getting off the bus and one of my candy bars dropped. I bent over to pick up the chocolate, and I felt a big, strong hand rub across my ass. Not again! I thought as I threw the candy down and ran off the bus. I didn't stop running until my front door was locked and my back was pressed against its hard frame.

For the next few fall months, I walked a little over five miles to and from school. Rain or shine, I did not care, as long as I was nowhere near Mr. Earl. I could not risk being taken advantage of anymore and having my feelings crushed by another grown man.

Then, one day, I stayed back for study hall in the library to study for my earth science test the following Monday. The aroma of the stale book pages filled the room. Kids with dust allergies were coughing and sneezing, and the chaperone teachers, who had gotten duped into doing this, patrolled the library. I chose a lonely round table in the back. I took out my earth science book and began to read when I got a visitor.

"Is this seat taken?"

I looked up, and, to my surprise, I saw Scarlet Waters. Scarlet was a freshman like me, and she was an African-American female on the volleyball team. Today, she had on a dark blue denim miniskirt, some leather over-the-knee boots, and a long-sleeved tee. I hadn't been spoken to by any of my peers in so long that I was speechless.

"Martin made me stay back for detention because I don't look presentable," she said as she sat down. She didn't introduce herself. She didn't have to; everybody knew who Scarlet was.

"M-m-m-martin?"

"Martin…Mr. Martin, our principal. I refuse to put a title on his name. Anyway, what are you here for?"

I lifted my book to show her the cover. "Studying,"

"Cool. You smart?"

"Well, I guess. But, then again, if I wasn't, would I tell you I wasn't?"

She smiled. "You right. You right."

I smiled and looked down at my book, but I could still feel her staring at me.

"So, you the kid, huh?"

"The kid?"

"Yeah, the one with AIDS?"

My mouth dropped.

"Oh, I'm cool with it! Don't think I'm judging you or anything. I knew someone who died of AIDS last summer."

My eyes got wide with the thought of the accusation.

"But I'm over it now. Well, not really. You never get over— "

"I don't have AIDS!"

"Shhhh!" one of the teachers hushed us from about ten feet away.

Scarlet barked back at her, "Shhhh, ya damn self! And keep ya shushing up dere and outta our conversation!" She gave the teacher a look and then looked back at me. "Whaddya mean you don't have AIDS? It's going all around school that somebody saw you and Gay Tommy having butthole pleasures in the gym, and—" She stopped talking when she saw my head drop.

"I may be gay, but I'd never mess with a guy who calls himself Gay Tommy."

Scarlet laughed. Gay Tommy was a skinny boy that was about 5'2". He was dark-skinned, and, no matter the weather, he wore a V-neck shirt, skinny jeans, and flip flops. But he was different from me. I like being a guy, but I like men. He liked acting like he was a girl and liked men. Before he spoke, he would put on lip gloss… every time, he wanted to talk. His lips were dripping wet all the time, and it was an embarrassment to gay men everywhere.

"It's true what they say. You can't believe everything you hear."

We both laughed. For the next hour, I listened to Scarlet talk and, occasionally, cuss out a passing teacher when they shushed her for laughing too hard. At 4:45, all of the after-school activities were over, and we both headed for the bus ramp. You would have thought I was King Kong and Scarlet was the skinny white lady. Everyone parted ways in the hallway to make room for us as if we were damned with the plague. The rest of the school had exiled me to be the one everyone could joke about, but Scarlet, she didn't participate in the taunts. For some reason, she saw me as…me, not gay, but as a human.

"Well, I'm going to walk to the neighborhood across the street 'cause I drove." She looked at the peering eyes and then back at me. "You want a ride?"

I didn't want to overstep my boundaries, seeing as how I'd just met her, so I said, "No, I'm fine,"

"Okay." She grabbed my phone and put her number in it. "I don't trust these niggas…" We looked at a short girl walking past, staring. "Or bitches! So call me if you ever… need to talk."

I knew that was code for "call me if you ever need me to beat anybody up." Scarlet was cute, but everybody knew she could kick ass. I got on the bus, and the first person I saw was the bus driver, Mr. Earl. Oh, God, no, I thought as I turned to take Scarlet up on her offer, but she was already out of sight. The sun was already starting to set, and I knew I would be caught in the darkness if I started walking. This couldn't be possible. The daily bus drivers don't drive the activity busses! I thought as I looked back at the older bus driver, and he had a shocked look on his face as if he thought he'd never see me again. And then, he smiled a little. I was frozen until a kid came up behind me and pushed me.

"Move, faggot!"

I sat in my designated seat behind the creepy, perverted bus driver. I was so scared. Then, I thought, He won't touch me; he'll lose his job. And, in this economy, who could afford that? Before I knew it, I was asleep with my head against the window.

When I woke up, the streetlights were shining brightly on me like spotlights, and the sun was almost lost in the purple sky.

I looked around, and I was the only one sitting in the green leather seats. My palms and the bottoms of my feet were sweating. My heart began to beat fast when I realized we were in Chesapeake City Park, a little over three miles away from my house. We came to a complete stop under a tree and a streetlight in the back of the parking lot. When the engine stopped, so did my heart. I closed my eyes and listened to the leather and springs in the seat squeak as Mr. Earl got up and stood and faced me.

"You don't know how long I've waited for this," he said as if we had planned this as a date. He caressed my face, and every goose bump on my body rose and every hair pricked up. "Coach Krisby is my neighbor and, also, a drunk. About a month ago, he came over and spilled a lot of delicious information." I opened my eyes as he sat in the seat across from me. "See, he never wanted to fuck a little boy. Oh, no! But even though he felt like pure shit after each time, he could not deny how good it felt. There was no way I was going to let my opportunity pass." He put his hand on my knee. "I've been checking you out, and you are one hot piece of ass." He stood up and started unbuckling his pants. "Now Krisby said you like it rough, but I'm going to treat you really good." Mr. Earl reached for my belt buckle, and I flinched. "It's okay. I won't hurt you."

I let him unbuckle my pants, and I lifted my ass, so he could pull my jeans and plaid boxers down. He looked at my soft and small penis and smiled. "I know you're nervous, but I'm about to change all of that." He began to jerk me off. Then, he shoved all of me in his mouth. I was still soft, but his mouth was so warm. I had never had anyone put their mouth on me before, and the feeling was unbelievable.

Within a couple bobs of his head, my once-soft cock was now at a full seven-inch erection. I leaned back on the leather with the back of my head resting on the window. His right hand followed the path of his lips going up and down my shaft. I could feel him wiggle his tongue around in my penis hole before withdrawing it back into his mouth to savor my taste. He looked up intently into my eyes, and we both let out a sigh of satisfaction. Then, I felt him moaning around my dick, swirling his tongue around my head as he sucked me in deeper.

"Oh, fuck," I groaned, pushing my dick into the back of his throat. "I can't wait to stick this thing in your ass." Listen to me, talking dirty, I thought.

My dirty words must have turned Earl on even more because he began bobbing his head up and down faster and faster. Reaching down with one hand, I grabbed a handful of salty brown hair and watched as his mustache seemed to make my cock disappear and reappear. I moaned my satisfaction, and Earl stopped sucking and started jerking.

"You like that?" He sucked once. "Huh?" Another suck. "You ready for me to fuck that tight asshole?"

I nodded, and he lifted my legs above my head and put my knees in my chest. Then, he bent down and kissed me.

"I'm going to make this the happiest night of your life."

I don't know why, but that turned me on. He stood up, and I watched him spit on my asshole. He slowly put his index finger in and out of my hole. "Ooh, that is tight!" He spat on my hole again, and, after two tugs of his manhood, he placed it on top of my hole. Then, he slowly put it in. "Does that hurt?"

I just looked him in his eyes and licked my lips. He grabbed the back of my head and pumped in and out of me. I grabbed at the seats, moaning and groaning. He bent down and kissed me and licked my young lips. I could feel his thick mustache tickling my nose and upper lip. I grabbed my penis and began to pull at it with one hand and rub my balls with the other. He grabbed my legs, using them to aid him in forcing my hole wider and wider with his penis, and, with each thrust, his bottom lip trembled until he had an orgasm right inside my hole. His whole face turned red with embarrassment. I just looked at him. I'm sure he was only inside me for five minutes.

"I'm sorry. It's just...You are so cute, and I've wanted this for a very long time. But the night's not over." He pulled out of me and got on all fours in the other seat. "It's your turn to fuck me."

What? I had never been the fucker, always the fuckee. But I stood up and stared at this grown man with his face down and his ass up.

"It's okay. Take your time."

I put my head at the entrance, and he exhaled deeply. I put it in and let out a groan myself. Everything inside him was gripping my dick. I fucked him vigorously, feeling the cum he left inside me drip and spread in between my ass cheeks. I was enjoying every stroke, every thrust. I grabbed at his hips, and sweat seemed to pour from the top of my head down my face until it drenched my shirt. I made all sorts of crazy faces, and I knew I looked like a special ed kid enjoying his first time.

Mr. Earl reached his hand back, and I could feel his rough fingertips reaching for my balls. Every time I went deep inside his ass, his fingers danced on my naked ball sack. My toes gripped the inside of my shoes, and I laid on his back, allowing his shirt to soak up my sweat as I reached my hand around and found his cock.

I began to beat his muscle, and he moaned out really loud, "Ahhh! Oh, yes! Fuck!"

I could feel him growing in my hand, and I watched him grip the seat as he kept moaning out curse words. His legs shook, and the dip in his back got deeper.

Finally, he let out an "Aaaaaauuuggh…shiiit!" He let lose an orgasm that scared the shit out of me.

I lifted up off of his back and kept plowing his asshole while he pulled all of the cum out of his dick. Watching the white goo drip off the seat and the wall, I felt my eruption coming. I lost my rhythm and just started pumping any kind of way till I exploded deep inside that man's ass. I came so much that, when I kept pushing in, cum poured out. I removed myself and watched my cum drip from his ass and down his balls. We cleaned up, and, unlike Coach Krisby, he held me, and we laid in the back seat of the bus. We talked and laughed and stared at the streetlight that shone so brightly on the two of us.

Then, Mr. Earl said, "I may be an old man, but I know I want you and need you in my life." I looked back at him. He continued, "I feel kind of childish saying this, but will you be my boyfriend?"

I laughed. "Yeah!"

Then, we kissed and continued talking. I liked Earl because he didn't want to just fuck. He liked to take me out, and, some days, when his wife wasn't home, he let me stay over at his house. Sometimes, for fun, he would sneak me into the guest bedroom when his old lady was asleep, and we'd make love there. The suspense made it more exciting, so I didn't mind sneaking in a grown man's window.

Then, one day, after one of our afternoon rendezvous, he said, "You know how Krisby told me about you? Well, I've been talking a lot about you, too, and I got some friends who would…you know…like to try you out."

Try me out? As if I was a new car…I just looked at him.

Kathryn

Today was a day like any other. The house was empty, and I had nothing to do, so I went to the local Office Max where I did my printing to ask them about a new project I was doing. When I ran my errands, I didn't feel like dressing up, so I usually wore my Redskins jersey, a baseball cap, and some sweats. That day, I put on my usual and some lipstick, hoping that that would help people to not think I was gay or anything. Then, I got in my car and drove on over.

The automatic doors slid open, and the smell of fresh paper greeted me. I had no need for anything else in the store, so I went straight to the printing counter. At the counter, a young boy about my daughter's age came up to help me. He was about 6'2" tall with dark chocolate skin and the prettiest teeth I had ever seen in my life. His hair was kind of low with waves, and the sides and the back were tapered. He had a goatee, and, through his jet black work shirt, I could see his chest poking out, showing that he worked out…regularly.

"Hey! You're a Redskins fan?"

"Yes, I am!"

"High five!" We high-fived each other over the counter. "Did you watch the game on Sunday?"

"Actually, no, I didn't."

"What? And you call yourself a fan?"

"Well, I was busy on Sunday, so I couldn't watch," I lied. I only watched the Redskins when they played my sister's team, the Cowboys. I think I only liked them because, when I was a kid, my father liked them, but I didn't really watch sports.

"Aw, man. Good game, though. Well, what can I do for you today?"

"Well, I was wondering if I could see your heaviest paper."

"Sure." He pulled out the paper. I felt it and played with it, and he must have noticed my face because he asked, "Is that what you're looking for?"

"No, I'm making church fans, so I need something kind of heavy but not too heavy."

"Okay. Let me see what I can find." He went back to his paper stack and brought out another piece of paper. "Okay. This is 120 pound paper. This might be better."

I did my usual feel test. "Oh, this is perfect!"

"Cool. So did you want me to print something out for you?"

"Not today. I just needed to make sure you guys had it."

"Okay. Well, feel free to come back anytime."

"Thank you." I left and went back to my lonely home.

By the next week, it was time for me to print, and I got dressed and went back to Office Max. This time, I had my hair and makeup done, and I was wearing my leopard print dress with the 3/4 length sleeves. The dress pulled in the middle, separating and hugging my breasts. It was what I liked to call "sexy conservative."

After my three-inch pumps made their first appearance through the double doors, I walked over to the printing counter and saw that the same boy was there, working.

"Well, hello there! Don't you look nice today?"

"Thank you. Well, I'm actually ready to print today."

I handed him the flash drive, and he started working. As the papers came off the printer, he handed them to me, and I went to the work station and began cutting off the white border. When I glanced up, I noticed the boy staring at me. I thought nothing of it, and, then, when he brought more papers for me to cut, he smiled, flashing those pretty teeth, and his eyes were low. I just politely smiled back and continued working, but, since he was staring, I decided I might as well put on a show.

From then on, whenever I needed something across the table, I bent all the way over and let out a small moan. The teasing got a reaction every time! Out of my peripheral vision, I would see his head jerk to look at me every time I moaned. I must admit, I enjoyed the attention. I was lacking so much of it from my own home. I finished cutting an hour after he finished printing. I walked over to the counter.

"I think I'm ready now," I said.

He came over to me, and I could see the shape of his penis in his pants. I smiled and continued, "I never knew cutting paper could take so long."

"Well, I'm something of a perfectionist, so my hands don't move as fast as your big machine does, shooting off."

He smiled widely. Then, he quickly lowered his head and rang me up. "That will be $10.25."

I looked at him; I knew that wasn't right. I had 250 double-sided color copies on this expensive paper.

He kept smiling. "I gave you the entrepreneurial discount."

"Oh, well, thank you…" I looked at his nametag. "Robbie."

"No problem, Ms…"

"Matos. Kathryn Matos." He looked confused. Of course, I didn't look mixed with my white skin and brown hair. "My husband is Latino."

His face sank in. "Oh, you're married?"

"Yeah."

I must have sounded weird when I said it because he said, "Oh, you're not happy?"

"Well, Robbie, one day you're going to get married, and you'll learn that every day isn't going to be a happy one. But you take a vow before God and a whole lot of witnesses to stay together, so you do. Basically, the only way I can describe it is…marriage can be the shit or *the shit*."

"Oh. Well, does he take you out?"

"Sometimes." I looked at his curious face. "Why?"

"Well, maybe I can take you out sometime."

I laughed. "Robbie, my husband is a preaching psychopath. If he found out, we'd both be dead!" I laughed. "Plus, I'm faithful." I slid my card for my purchase, and he handed me a receipt.

"Well, Mrs. Matos, a group of friends and I like to go to Applebee's on Kempsville after nine on the weekends. If you ever get bored, you can come, sit, and eat with us."

I smiled. "We'll see, Robbie." I walked out.

Kempsville Road? I live off Kempsville Road. In fact, Applebee's sits across from my neighborhood, making my street reek of steak and other goodies, I thought.

That night, I put on some smooth jams, cleaned the whole house, and lit every candle I had. When José came in from work, I was standing on the bed butt naked with my red heels on and my hair tossed all over my head.

He laughed. "Mami, what are you doing?"

"What does it look like? I'm setting the mood."

He walked over to the bed. Then, he picked me up off of the bed and stood me on the floor in front of him.

"We lost the romance, baby, and I want it back."

He kissed me while his big arms brought me close to him.

"I love you," he whispered.

"I love you, too."

He laid me down on the bed and kissed me long and hard. In one quick motion, his pants were down to his knees, and he was penetrating me.

"Wait! Slow down!"

He did, for about five strokes, and then he was power-driving me again. I preferred going slow, but he was good either way. He put one of my breasts in his mouth and teased my nipple with his tongue. Then, he put his face in my neck, breathing heavily. I dug my nails in his back, and he whispered, "I'm 'bout to cum."

"No, baby, just a little longer!"

Then, he let out a deep groan, and I just laid there, hoping the night wasn't over. He kissed me and rolled over.

"Is that it?"

"Baby, I been working all day. I'm tired."

I just stared at him. Then, he held me and said, "You know I love you, right?" and, before I could answer, he was snoring in my ear.

At two a.m., I was still up. I went to the window and stared at the glowing Applebee's sign. The restaurant was obviously closed, but the sign's light shone so brightly. I laid back in bed with the three minute man and just stared at him. I remembered nights when sleep wasn't an option, when sheets were covered in sweat and other bodily fluids, and my body shook so much from multiple orgasms that I thought I was having a seizure. I remembered being so happy I couldn't wait to marry him. Now, look at me, I thought as I got out of bed again—this time, with my vibrator— and headed for my office floor. One thing was for sure: if he wouldn't do the job, B.O.B. would.

****

"Hey, what time are you coming home tonight? Well, I thought maybe we could have a date night…But it's Friday night. Remember when we had fun on Friday nights? Okay…uh huh…all right, bye."

Another night without my husband. Well, he'd be home, but I wouldn't be. I refused to be forty-five and living like an old maid. It was only six o'clock, and he had already made up in his mind that he was going to bed as soon as he got home. B.O.B. had died, so I decided to get some exercise and walk to Walgreens to get some batteries. As I walked across the street, the aroma of onions, bell peppers, and cooked meats filled the air, and I thought, Maybe I could stop by after nine for some half-priced appetizers.

That night, I put on my navy blue pantsuit with a coral shirt underneath, and then I put on some heels.

"Where you goin'?" José asked. He was lying in the bed, eating cookies and ice cream and watching bootleg movies. It was 9:30 p.m., and he had told me he was going to be so tired, yet he hadn't gone to sleep yet!

"Applebee's. I want to get one of those five hundred calorie meals. You want to come?"

"Naw, you go ahead."

Of course, he didn't want to come. That would require him to actually spend some time with me…bastard.

I walked over to the restaurant and was greeted by a young, thin hostess. The lighting was dim, and the smell of assorted delectables filled the dining room. Every flat screen TV had one of the ESPN channels on, and the bar was full of men drinking and shouting at nearby tables.

"How many, ma'am?"

"Oh, uh, just one."

"Okay. Would you like to sit at the bar?"

"Sure."

The lady handed me a menu, and I walked over to the bar.

Before I could sit down, I heard, "Mrs. Matos!"

I looked up, and there was Robbie with a table full of young people. His face was bright, and he was clearly happy to see me because he leaned forward, waving so hard that he almost knocked everyone's drinks over. I smiled and waved back.

Jen

I think it was safe to say that Charlotte was my girlfriend. We talked about everything. I asked her if my mom knew she was gay, and she answered with a simple yes. I was going to ask her if they had done anything together, but I didn't want to know. Charlotte, also, told me that she wasn't one hundred percent gay; she was bi. This meant that, every now and then, she liked to visit her fuck buddy when she wanted the real thing. She, also, said that she'd had her heart broken ten years ago, so she was reluctant to have a proper relationship. I tried to think of who it could've been. Ten years ago, I was thirteen. It must have been Uncle Kadeem. I had started calling him uncle

67

because he and Charlotte were inseparable for about four years.

She obviously saw my face drop when she said the thing about the relationship, and she pulled my face close to hers, kissed me, and said, "Jen, I have wanted you for a long time, and I am saying to you now, 'I want you to be my girlfriend for as long as you want me!'"

I didn't know what to say. Of course, I had wanted her badly, but was it just a crush or hormones? Obviously not, because I thought about her every minute of every day. Even when she hugged me, I could feel myself getting excited just from her touch.

We came to the conclusion that my age would cause all types of problems with my mom, so we discussed how we could make it work. We both truly wanted that to be the case. We, also, talked about Charlotte's insatiable appetite for sex and her needs for new and exciting times, but she kept strongly emphasizing loyalty. The ideas that she told me about and the stories of her past got me so horny that I begged her to eat me out before she finished the conversation. She laughed and told me of three or more girls at once in bed, lesbian parties, bi-sexual orgies, and so many other stories. I was nervous about doing that kind of stuff, but, if she was with me, I would be willing to try it one day…maybe.

The first six weeks of my relationship with Charlotte were like heaven and hell. When I was with her, she made me feel so loved and special. But, when we were apart, I felt like my heart was breaking, and I was always trying to find any excuse to go to her house. My mom started to get concerned that I might be getting on Charlotte's nerves by being around all the time, but Charlotte told her that she loved having me there like a little sister and that I was welcome 24/7.

Our lovemaking just got better every time we did it, and, after two weeks, we very happily proclaimed that we were in love. I knew I had been in love with Tony, but this, this was bigger than some heterosexual thing. Whenever I looked into Charlotte's eyes, my stomach fluttered, and I just wanted to grab her and not let go. What was so weird was that we had started to talk a lot about orgies and group sex, and I didn't feel any jealousy at all. But just the thought of myself being naked in front of a bunch of people I didn't know had me on edge. I know that sounds immature, but look at how long it took me to take a shower in front of her.

Another problem we had was trying to play it cool in front of my parents. Charlotte would come over, and I'd sit on one side of the couch, and she'd sit on another, and we'd try not to look at each other, or not look at each other for too long. There was one time when we sat next to each other and neither of us noticed that we were holding hands, and I was so comfortable with her being next to me that, when I got up to get some water, I kissed her on the lips! I looked around quickly and saw that Mike was asleep and that Mom's eyes were glued to the movie on the television. Whew!

Every year, our neighbors threw their annual Halloween costume party, and, ever since I'd turned nineteen, I'd been going. This year, Charlotte and I decided to go as slutty Catwoman twins. We got dressed in my room, and, when we went downstairs, my mom almost had a conniption. Charlotte and I both had on skintight black leather tights that we had cut up and over-the-knee leather boots. Our tops were leather bras, and I had on black leather gloves that came up almost to my shoulders, and Charlotte had biker gloves. Her hair was parted down the middle into two afro puffs, and my hair was slicked back into a ponytail. We each had on eye masks that tied behind our heads, and the icing on the cake was our whips.

Mom's eyes were so wide that I thought her eyeballs would fall out of their sockets. "Where are the rest of your outfits?"

"What do you mean 'the rest'?" I asked.

"Well, it looks like you might have accidentally cut some of it off."

Charlotte and I laughed. "Mom, it's supposed to look like this."

"Oh, well, you hadn't planned on wearing that to the Johansons', had you?"

Charlotte and I looked at each other. Then, she said, "Well, yeah, Kat."

I could see in my mom's eyes that she wanted to say something so badly, but the fact that I was not a little girl anymore prohibited her every time. She exhaled deeply before saying, "All right," and then she went back to looking at the computer.

The two of us walked two houses down to the Johansons', and Mrs. Johanson answered the door dressed as a Viking princess. She had a gold Viking crown on her head, and she wore an orange corset and a long white skirt with two inch wide gold satin ribbon trim. Across her shoulders was a gold cape with orange ribbon accents.

"Hello! Welcome!" She was clearly intoxicated. "Oh, you two are the most adorable things! Come in! Be merry! There's liquor in the kitchen!"

As we walked through the house, heads turned, and the whispering began. I couldn't make out all of it, but I could hear some.

"Who is that?"

"Look at those…"

"I would put so much dick in her…"

"Jen?"

That one I heard clearly and knew all too well. I turned around to the Incredible Hulk or, without a costume, Tony. Tony was naturally super strong with bulging muscles. Whenever he was out in public, people stopped and stared at how big his arms and chest were.

"Hey! What are you doing here?"

"I was invited."

"By who? I invited you two years in a row, and you said it wasn't for you." He just looked at me. That meant he didn't want to tell me. "Well?"

"Well, what?"

"Who invited you?" He just laughed. "Or who are you here with?"

"Man, anyway…"

He walked away.

Bastard. But I found Charlotte again. We got some drinks and tried to guess who was under each costume. The best thing about these parties was that everyone was anonymous. We kept drinking, and she kept whispering nasty, delicious stuff in my ear all night, and I had to go to the bathroom twice to wipe myself!

When I came out of the bathroom again, I heard, "Jen?"

This time, it was a female. I turned to see the sluttiest Girl Scout I'd ever seen. It was my best friend since eighth grade, Paris Chao. She was black and Asian. Her dad was…well, I don't know what he was—Chinese, Japanese, or Korean—but he was Asian, and her mom was black. She wore a green beret, and she had her black hair spiral-curled, so the curls bounced on her shoulders. She had on a low-cut white tie top. It had green trim on the sleeves, and it stopped right below her breasts. She had on the shortest green pleated skirt that teased the eye. I was pretty sure every guy was waiting for her to either bend over or just move a little too fast. And, lastly, she had on white knee highs and black heels and a green sash with "Cookie Girl" printed in gold on it.

"Hey, Paris."

"It's about time you got here! Is Charlotte with you?"

"Yeah, why?"

"'Cause Tony's here with tacky Mrs. Clause." Paris very obviously pointed to Mrs. Clause.

Her butt was so humongous that her dress didn't even cover it. She had on black fishnet stockings, and we could blatantly see her red velour thong with white fur on the top. Her too small, too tight dress was low-cut, and her ginormous breasts looked like they were fighting to burst out of the opening. She had on what looked like six-inch high, bright red, over-the-knee leather boots with buckles up the side, and she wore a curly half wig that flowed down her back and a red headband. But her natural hair, which was showing in the front, was nappy and thin, and, to make her look even more like a stereotype, she had on the longest fake nails I'd ever seen in my life.

"That's what he left you for? Bitch…ugly and ghetto."

I just shook my head, and we walked back to Charlotte. I had told Paris about my new lover, but the two had never met.

"Hey, babe. This is my best friend Paris. Paris, this is Charlotte."

"Hi."

Charlotte got up and hugged her. "Hey, baby."

For the rest of the night, we drank and flirted with guys and laughed. Paris got so drunk that she tripped, and her breasts fell out of her shirt. We laughed so hard, and then she picked up her tits and waved them in my face.

"Hello, Jen," she said in her Mickey Mouse voice. "I think you should help me back in my shirt!"

I laughed, but, on the inside I was thinking, I've seen Paris naked plenty of times, but I've never touched her naked! I picked up each perfect breast and put them back into her shirt.

She bit her bottom lip, smiled, and said, "Thanks!" before walking away.

I was about to think that that was weird until Charlotte came up behind me and whispered, "Why didn't you ask me for help?"

"Huh?"

"She's sexy as hell!"

I quickly elbowed her in the ribs. "Shut up!"

As the party went on, I couldn't stop thinking about touching my friend's naked breasts. I must have started daydreaming because I jumped when Charlotte came up behind me and grabbed my ass. When I realized that no one was around, I quickly turned around and kissed her on the lips. Only it wasn't Charlotte…it was Paris!

"Oh, God! I'm sorry, Paris. I thought you were Charlotte."

"Hey! It's okay. Charlotte wouldn't mind you kissing your best friend, would she? I mean, it's not like we fucked, is it?" The more she talked, the more I realized how drunk she was. "I mean, it's not like we did this." She grabbed the back of my head and gave me a deep tongue kiss!

When she pulled away, I didn't know what to say. "Wow, Paris! You really are a good kisser. But you've had more practice than me."

I expected her to laugh at our usual humor, but her eyes filled with tears, and she said, "Fuck you, Jen!" Then, she left the party.

I rushed to find Charlotte to tell her what happened.

"Relax. I'll find her. Keep your phone handy. I'll text you." Then, she disappeared out the door.

I tried entertaining myself by watching Mrs. Clause talk to the Joker, a burglar, and Tarzan. Where was the Hulk? If that would have been me, the three men would have been thrown across the room, and I would have been cursed out. No doubt Tony was a little psycho, and crazy mixed with super strength was a terrible combination. I looked around, and there was the Hulk by the punch bowl, drinking and staring at me.

Just then, my phone vibrated, and it was Charlotte. Her text read, "Meet me in the BB&T parking lot." I looked back at Tony, who was still staring and now walking toward me.

"Hey, lady."

"Hey." I looked at Mrs. Clause. "Your bitch needs a leash. That's not a good look."

He smiled. "She's a stupid hoe."

"But you're with her, so what does that make you?" He shrugged his shoulders. "Well, enjoy your new girlfriend." I started to walk away.

"She ain't my girlfriend."

I kept walking.   BB&T sat right in front of my house. I walked over and met the two girls.

"Jen," Charlotte started, "Paris wants to watch us have sex."

My mouth dropped. I stared at them both, trying to see if this was some practical joke. But they both just kept smiling at me. My life had been completely changed ever since I'd turned over this new gay leaf. "Um, what?"

74

"Paris loves you because you guys have been friends for so long, but now she's curious about being gay and thinks that, if she watches you have sex, it will help make up her mind about being gay, straight, or bi."

I looked at them both. "No offense, but what the fuck? Paris, can't you just watch a fuckin' porno like I did?" Tears came into her eyes again. "Oh, boo hoo!"

"I told you she wouldn't understand."

Then, Charlotte stepped in. "Jen! Don't be a bitch!"

"Well, it's a little too late for that, Charlotte!"

I turned and started walking to my house when Charlotte grabbed me and whispered, "Remember I told you I needed this in a relationship?"

"And do you remember when I said I might be interested, but wasn't comfortable?"

She gave me a confused look. "I can't be in a relationship with a close-minded person."

"Oh, trust me. You don't have to be."

Her face brightened. "Okay then. So my place?"

I shook my head. "Fuck off, Charlotte."

Boy Toy

One day, after school, I was in the library getting some studying done at my usual table in the back corner of the library. I was surrounded by bookcases, and there was no way anybody could see me unless they were looking for me. I was reading my history book when someone came back by my table. I assumed they were just looking for a book, so I kept my head down. But I couldn't help but get the feeling I was being stared at. I jerked my head to get my hair out of my face, and, when I looked up, I saw Martin Luke staring at me.

"What?"

"You're the faggot. You tell me."

"What? What are you talking about?"

Martin pulled a chair out and sat in it backwards. "I see the way you look at me. You think I'm hot."

"I don't use the term hot."

"Well, give me a word you would use to describe me."

"Um…I don't know."

"Take your time and think about it."

I didn't know where he was going with it, but I started thinking. "Um, tall."

"Tall is a good one. Give me another one."

"Um." I looked at his hair. "Dreads."

"Aw, come on! Those are easy ones. Give me something else."

I laughed nervously. "I really don't know."

"Really?" He smiled and stood up, flexing his muscles. "No other word comes to mind when you see me?"

"Uh, big, I guess."

He stopped and smiled at me. "That's the word I was looking for. Let me show you how big I am."

"What?" I was confused, but I was even more confused when he whipped this really big penis out of his basketball shorts. I laughed nervously again. "You should put that up, Martin. People might think you're gay."

"Naw, that's not gonna happen. But you know what is?"

"What?"

"You're gonna suck this."

"What? No!"

"Oh, yes, you are." He started walking toward me. "You like sucking dick, don't you?"

I shook my head violently.

"Yes, you do. Come on." He reached his hand out slowly to grab the back of my head, but I swatted at it. "Don't fight it."

I kept hitting his hands and arms, but he was stronger than me. He grabbed a handful of my hair and pulled my head back. He was stroking himself as he looked me in my eyes.

"Now, you be a good faggot and suck it good. No teeth." He put his penis at my lips, but I didn't open my mouth. He slapped his dick on my face. "C'mon. Open up."

A tear rolled down my cheek. Next thing I knew, Martin was in the air, then on the ground. I looked up, and Scarlet was on top of my oppressor. She had his penis in one hand, his balls in the other, and her left foot in his right armpit. Martin was making all types of faces.

"The next time," Scarlet stated, "I see your penis anywhere out and about, I will rip it clean off! Do you hear me?"

"Yeah," Martin grunted.

Scarlet twisted the penis. "What was that?"

"Yeah!" Martin yelled out.

"Shhh!" we heard a teacher say.

Scarlet let go of the boy. "Fix yo' nasty ass up and get outta here!"

Martin hopped up, put his dick in his pants, and ran away.

Scarlet looked at me. "So, you were just gonna let him do that to you?"

I put my head down. "He's stronger than me."

"He may be, but you can still defend yourself. Look at me."

I picked my head up.

"I will always have your back. But, sometimes, you got to have your own."

Kathryn

It was the second night that I was driving home, both satisfied and ashamed. That night at Applebee's, Robbie introduced me to all of his college friends.

"This is Macy; she's a nursing major. Nathan is studying business, and Clarence wants to be a lawyer, but he goes to Regent with us for now." They all waved politely, and I sat down.

"So, Mrs. Matos," Nathan started, "what do you do, if you don't mind me asking?"

"Oh, of course not. I own my own printing business. I print just about anything."

"I actually saw some fans she designed. They were pretty cool, different from anything I've seen."

"Fans?" Macy asked.

"Yes, like church fans," I replied.

"Oh, so you print for churches?"

"Churches, funeral homes, all types of companies and organizations."

"That's cool."

We talked for hours. It was so nice to talk to some educated, young people who actually knew what they wanted to do with their lives and didn't just want to drink and smoke weed all day. At one a.m., we all said goodbye, and I started to cross the parking lot when Robbie ran up to me.

"Mrs. Matos! Um, I really enjoyed talking to you tonight."

"So did I, Robbie."

"Well, uh, I was wondering if you would like to finish our conversation at my place? I stay in Crosswinds right up the street."

I didn't know why I said yes, but I did, and, soon, I was in his living room, talking about everything. The one thing that had attracted me to José was his mind. He was so smart, and he had taught me so much. But now, since he seemed to hate talking, he just said, "I dunno" all the time. So talking to Robbie was like biting into a candy bar I hadn't had in a long time.

"You know, Mrs. Matos, I've been thinking a lot about what we talked about in the store that day."

"I'm sorry?"

"You know, when you said that marriage can either be the shit or *the shit*. And I've been thinking, you must be in *the shit* stage."

"Oh?"

"Well, yeah, because when you talk about marriage, your face gets real sad, but, when you talk about your husband, your face lights up." He smiled; I laughed. "But you only talk about the old times between you two." I looked in his eyes. "It's clear you're in love with the guy you met and maybe even the guy you married, but you're not attracted to the man you sleep in the same bed with at night."

My mouth dropped. "Wow, and how old are you?"

"I'm twenty-three." He smiled. "And I am incredibly attracted to you."

"What? You don't even know me."

"But I want to get to know you."

"Oh, my goodness!" I stood up. "I should go."

He stood. "Just listen to me." I didn't move. "Sometimes, you marry the wrong person. Does that mean you rob your heart of what it desires? You thought he was the one that completed you, and you married him, but he dropped the ball." He came closer to me and grabbed my arms. "I'm just asking that you let me pick it up." Then, he leaned in and kissed me.

It felt so good, and I could feel myself giving in, but I pushed away. "Robbie, I have kids your age."

"Kathryn, age is just a number."

"Don't call me that! And not to me, it's not." I grabbed my coat. "I have to go."

"Wait!"

I stopped.

"If you won't let me love you, let me, at least, show you what you're missing."

"Robbie, stop!"

"He can't love you the way I can!" He was yelling. "And he probably doesn't make love to you at all. I bet he doesn't even take his clothes all the way off for you." I looked at him, and he lowered his voice. "How much money are you going to waste on batteries?"

I walked over to him and smacked him right in his face. "Shut up!"

He grabbed me and kissed me. I pulled away and tried to slap the taste out of his mouth. He looked at me, and I stared at him. I was breathing hard, and I could feel my heart beating so hard and loud that I thought it was vibrating the walls.

"I'm sorry." He got his car keys. "I'll take you home."

I stomped out of the apartment and into his waiting car. When we got to the intersection of Providence Road and Indian River Road, I said, "Keep straight."

"What?"

I just looked at him, and he followed my directions. "Pull in here."

We pulled over into this small office park. "Cut off the car," I told him, and he did. "Listen, I'm sorry. But I'm married, and—"

His lips cut me off as he kissed me, and, this time, I didn't stop him. I didn't want to. We made love for over an hour in the back seat of his car, and, boy, did it feel good. He did things I had forgotten about. He did things I thought he had made up. He made parts of my body vibrate and quiver and jolt, and I could do nothing but release all of my frustrations through my cum.

We had pushed the front seats up as far as they could go, and we both got in the back seat. Robbie kissed me as he helped me out of my clothes. Once I was completely naked, I bent over the center console, and Robbie began to eat my vagina out from the back. He rubbed my butt as he moved his tongue around my clitoris, something I had never experienced before. I gripped the steering wheel and the gear shift as he grinded his face into my wet vagina. He took his tongue and moved it in and out of my hole and then licked up to my butthole. He licked in little circles before putting his tongue in and out. I was screaming and shaking and didn't realize he had undone his pants.

Robbie grabbed my waist and pulled me down onto his hard penis. He was way bigger and harder than my husband

and a feeling I had never felt before shot through my body. I leaned back onto my lover, and he grabbed my breasts with one hand and wrapped his other arm around my waist. I buried my toes deep into the floor of the car as I pushed myself up and down on his hard penis. I was going slowly at first, but, as Robbie moved my body faster, I reached my arm around his head and kissed him as I bounced up and down.

"You like this?" he asked me.

"Uh huh," I managed to get out.

"Tell me you like it."

"I like this penis."

"Don't say penis, baby. Say you like this dick."

"I like this dick."

He grunted a little. "Say you love this dick."

"I love this dick, baby."

"You want me to cum inside you?"

"Yeah."

"Tell me."

"I want you to cum inside me, baby."

"Mmm. I want you to cum on this dick, baby."

I just moaned a little.

"You gon' cum for me, baby?"

"Yeah."

Our bodies moved together, and it wasn't long before we were both experiencing orgasms. I came on him, and he came inside me.

Tonight was the second night that I'd been with Robbie, and I found myself racing to beat my husband home. What am I thinking? I wondered as tried to snap back to reality. I'm married to José Matos. We met on January 25, 1980. We got married on September 9, 1987. We were madly in love, and...were? Did I say we were madly in love? I pulled into

82

the driveway of my home and looked at myself in the rearview mirror.

"I love José," I said aloud. "I'm in love with him." I sounded more like I was trying to convince myself, instead of believing it. I looked at my face, so heavy with confusion. Next thing I knew, I was being scared to death by a rapping on my window. It was Jen. I got out of the car. "What is wrong with you, crazy girl?"

"Nothing. Why are you sitting in the car looking crazy?"

"I can't have some alone time?"

"I guess so. I don't know." She unlocked the door, and we went in.

"So, what did you do all day?" I asked her.

"Nothing."

"You didn't hang out with Fish?"

"Nope."

"Paris?"

"Nope." I watched her while she tossed M&Ms in the air and tried to catch them in her mouth.

"So you just did nothing by yourself…all day?"

"Yup."

"Well, Jen, I've been meaning to ask you. When are you going back to school?"

"I don't know."

"Well, don't you think you need to know?"

"I mean, I'm not in a rush. I don't have a roommate in my room here, and Pops is like a personal chef. Life is good."

"Well, if you're going to stay here, why not put that degree to use and get a job and an apartment?"

"Mom, really, I'm fine."

"Well, I just thought, since you're never here and you're always staying over at a friend's house or *Fish's* house, that you'd want—"

"What was that?"

"What was what?"

"Why'd you say her name like that?"

"Like what?"

"Nothing." She got up and walked upstairs.

I really didn't think I'd said it in any particular way, but I did not like Jen hanging around Fish. That night, when we were watching the movie, I saw them kiss. And it wasn't a friendly kiss or a familial kiss or whatever other name you might give it to make it sound all right. It was a relationship kiss, and I nearly threw up in my mouth when I saw it; I was so disgusted. My best friend and my daughter kissing, in my house! And every time she went over there, I had to pretend like I didn't know. I knew! And I think Fish was living out some sick fetish! I've never forgotten the day she told me she was in love with me ten years ago.

It was July 31, 2001, and we were having Jen's thirteenth birthday party. José had invited his best friend, Ray, and his girlfriend, Simone, and I had invited Fish and her man, Kadeem. They had been dating for four years, and it was as if Kadeem was a part of our family. Jen had about five little girls over, and they were chasing the boys around with water guns. The guys and Simone were drinking beer and talking around the grill.

"Hey, babe!" I called to José. "Watch the kids while we go inside right quick."

He smiled and gave me a head nod. It seemed like he couldn't stop smiling those days. I had given him children, and every day was a happy day for him. I pulled Fish into the kitchen with me.

"Girl, you are glowing!" Fish said.

"Well, I guess I owe that to my children keeping me young."

"Or to the hard-working man that is apparently laying pipe every night."

I laughed and hit her on the arm. "Shut up!"

She smiled. "I want that."

"Aw, honey, you will have it very soon. I can feel it."

She reached into her pocket and pulled out a diamond ring. It had three big diamonds on it and made my wedding band look like a cheap piece of costume jewelry.

"Oh, my goodness, Fish! He proposed?"

She nodded.

"Did you say yes?"

She stared at me.

"Wait! Why is it not on your finger? Fish, you better not push this guy away! He's good for you." I turned and started to put icing on the cake. "You know I'm not going to keep standing by and watching you push men away. Now, Carl, he was bad. But Rick, Rick was— "

Then, she did the unthinkable. She kissed me right in my kitchen!

"I said no."

"What?" I didn't even acknowledge the kiss.

"Well, I didn't, but I will."

"Why? He's awesome."

"Yeah, he's sweet and kind and good and would do anything for me." She imitated him, "'I'm sorry, honey. I'll try not to let my heels hit the floor in that irritating manner anymore.' I could tell him that I want to chuck it all for a rice farm in Southeast Asia, and he'd be researching plane fares within the hour."

"So it seems to me that you have nothing to complain about."

"I'm not complaining, but why? Why is he so perfect? He won't argue with me. He won't even put up a fight."

"I think you should try to show a little appreciation."

"I'm losing my mind."

"I wish I could help you. I really do, but Kadeem and José are best friends, and you're my best friend."

"Yeah."

I looked up, and her face was almost as bright as the sun. "Yeah what?"

"I'm your best friend."

"Yeah, and…"

"You'd do anything for me?"

I stopped icing my cake and looked at her. "Okay, Fish, what are you driving at?"

"Marry me, Kat."

"What?"

"Let's run away to Vegas and get married!"

"You can't be serious!"

"Yes. Kadeem and I aren't made for each other, but you—"

"Are astonished!"

"Are my soulmate! We can get married and live together forever."

"It's not that simple."

"Why not?"

"Because I'm in love with José. Not to mention, I am not physically attracted to you."

"Liar!"

"What did you call me?"

"You're a liar! You've wanted me from the day we met."

"Oh, now I agree with you, Fish, you've gone over the deep end."

"Oh, so you mad now?"

"I'm not mad! I'm flabbergasted! To think that, with what I thought was a beautiful friendship over the years, you would come up with the insane notion that I…that we…I'm married, Charlotte!"

"I know!"

"And I'm in love with José!"

"I know."

"And not to mention, I am one hundred percent heterosexual."

"Ha! Is that what you tell yourself? What about Mystery Man?"

"What about him?"

"Don't act like you forgot the night we fucked each other crazy!"

"Whatever, Charlotte!"

"Whatever, Charlotte? Whatever, Charlotte? Excuse me, but was I or was I not the one you were sleeping with when José fucked up?" I walked into the living room, and she, of course, followed. "Oh, how quickly we forget the ones who were there for us."

"There for me?"

"Yes, bitch!"

"Oh! But how soon did you forget that I brought your naked ass in out of the cold! I was at the hospital with you during two alcohol poisonings!"

"You just keep bringing that up."

"Oh, no! I got more. How many times did I stop talking to you because you had an abortion? And how many times did I have to hide liquor, so you wouldn't drink while pregnant and you still had a miscarriage? Huh? Huh?"

Silence. "I was there for you when your parents died. I let you stay with me rent free for years." She had tears in her eyes. I picked her head up and said real low and slow, "So that pussy you gave me was owed to me. The least you could have done was spread your legs without complaining about it."

Then, she punched me so hard I fell to the floor. I had never been punched before, and I thought she had broken my jaw.

"Don't disrespect me, Kathryn Amber Wheeler! I will whoop yo' ass all up and down this Barbie and Ken dollhouse." She turned to leave, then stopped suddenly in her tracks, looked at me, and said, "I love your sorry ass. I'm actually in love with you. You don't think I don't feel profound jealousy every time José looks at you in that loving manner or that my heart doesn't skip a beat every time I see you, that my feelings couldn't possibly be real? What, Kathryn? What did you think?"

My face hurt so badly that I couldn't speak. I could feel the blood rushing so fast that my skin was burning.

"No answer? Well, you'll never have to see my black ass again."

Of course, we became friends again, but we went through a year of only seeing each other on special occasions. Well, Jen was an exact replica of me at her age, and I couldn't help but wonder if Fish was attracted to her for that exact reason. What was more disgusting was the fact that Fish had known Jen since birth. Jen was the daughter she never had, and now she was…ugh! But judging from the way Jen acted tonight, maybe that little thing was over. I wanted to say something, but my daughter was an adult, so what was there to say? My phone vibrated; it was a text from Robbie.

88

"When was the last time you screamed like that?" it read.

"Oh, it's been a while," I texted back before deleting both messages and going upstairs to shower.

Buzz. Buzz. "Send me a pic."

I laughed. This was so wrong. I shut the bathroom door and stripped down to my bra and underwear. Click. No. Click. Maybe. I tossed my hair and put my finger in my mouth. Click. Cute. Click. Yes! Click.

Bam! The bathroom door flew open and hit the wall. José was standing there, wearing today all over him. "What are you doing?"

"Well...uh...what does it look like I'm doing? I'm taking pictures for you. But you walked in, so...they're ruined."

"No, let me see." Before I could protest, my phone was in his hand. "Cute, babe." He analyzed each picture.

Buzz. Text message. Oh, my God! I grabbed the phone and his hand in one of mine and the back of his neck with another, and I kissed him. "Baby, let's shower together."

"Naw."

"Please!" I gave my puppy dog eyes. "Pwetty pwease!" He smiled. "No."

"José!"

"Kitty Kat!"

"Why not?"

"Because I just want to take a shower and go to sleep, and, if you get in the shower with me, then you're just going to want to play."

I went and sat on the bed and put my phone safely in my bra. "And how do you know that?"

"Know what?"

"That I'm going to want to play."

"'Cause you used to do it all the time."

"But not anymore…"

He just looked at me. "Baby, what do we do that we used to do?" He looked at his feet. "I'm going to take a shower." He went in the bathroom and shut the door.

I looked at my phone. The text was from my sister asking if she could swing by tomorrow. I deleted it.

José

I'm a barber and a pastor. People trust me to make sure they look good, and they trust me with their spiritual lives. I give inspiration and uplifting words all day, every day. At the shop, my chair is my pulpit, and, at the church, the podium is. Between the shop and the church, I don't really spend much time at home. My kids understand. When they want to see me, they just come to the barbershop or wait till I get home. My wife…she's a different story. She'll call me at random times of the day, but, not to say hey or see how I'm doing. No, she calls to remind me to bring home dishwashing liquid, bleach, or toilet paper. And what I can't stand is when she calls yelling at me if something has gotten cut off.

"José!"

"Huh?"

"Did you know that the water is off?"

"No, I didn't know that. I'm at work!"

"Okay, so what are you gonna do?"

See, that right there? That's what I don't like. If I am your husband, and I am the one paying the bills, don't call me yelling at me and talking down to me. I make sure that nobody in my house ever misses a meal, the lights stay on, the water stays running. If anything gets shut off, I make sure it's cut right back on. And do you know my wife never ever says thank you? My kids, especially my daughter, will tell me or text me randomly and say, "Thanks, Pops, for all you do. I appreciate you." Those are the things a man, a father, and a husband needs to hear, not the nagging and complaining that I get every day. You know, I am slowly becoming less and less attracted to my wife.

One day, not long after we had gotten married, I went to Hecht's, and I bought her four nice suits. I think I spent somewhere between three hundred and four hundred dollars. She saw the suits and smiled, but, as soon as she saw the price tags, she said, "Oh, no! You need to take these back and give me the money you spent. I can go to Marshall's and get ten suits and shoes to match for this!" She never said thank you.

Recently, I went to the Southern Hospitality Auto Group on Military Highway, and I bought her a hatchback Kia Forte for our anniversary. She looked at it, and I said, "What do you think?"

She said, "Who did you buy this for?"

As if there was anybody else I would buy a car for during our anniversary month. I kept my cool and said, "I bought it for you."

She walked around the car once and poked her lips out and just looked at it as if she didn't want to touch it.

I ignored the looks. "You want to take it for a test drive?"

She just shook her head.

It was getting harder and harder to be happy with someone who was clearly unhappy. "So, what do you think, Kathryn?"

"It looks like a soccer mom."

"A what?"

"It looks like something a soccer mom would drive."

"So, what are you saying? You don't want the car? You've been driving a '99 Ford Escort that breaks down all of the time. It's 2012 and this is a brand new 2013! Nobody's ever driven it!"

"I understand, and I get it, but..." She just shook her head. "This just doesn't look like me."

I could've went off and lost it, but I just put my head down, said, "Okay," and took the car back to the dealership. When my children found out, they called and texted me and told me that I was a great husband and father and that they appreciated me. I don't know what my son said to my wife, but I know she ended up crying about it. It's just little things like that that tear a man down. I try to do my best to be the best husband and be there for everyone, but it seems like whatever I do isn't good enough. Like I said earlier, I find myself feeling less and less attracted to Kathryn. When I come home, sure, I want to have sex. What man doesn't? But making love? That's something I just don't want to do with Kat anymore. I can't make love to her knowing that she doesn't look at me like a wife should. She doesn't try to encourage me. She doesn't stand behind me yelling, "You go, baby!" All I hear is, "Now what?"

You know what I want to tell her? "How 'bout you get a job instead of sitting home on the computer all day. How 'bout you do that, instead of calling me and telling me what's been cut off. Call me and tell me that you paid a bill. Tell me that!"

Don't get me wrong. I love my wife. I just don't know for how much longer.

Boy Toy

I remember the first party I went to. I was so nervous and scared. By my third party, I was calmer than ever. Earl and I got into his car and headed toward the Cottages at Great Bridge.

"You look great tonight," Earl said.

"Thank you," I replied.

I wore a pair of black skinny jeans, some black Vans, a black tee, and a black leather jacket that Earl had bought for me. I wasn't Goth or emo; I just looked good in black. We were quiet the whole way there. Earl always got quiet before the parties because he got so excited.

We turned on Bettes Way and pulled in front of the two-bedroom cottage. It was easy to spot which one we were going to because it was the only cottage with lights on. The Cottages at Great Bridge was a seniors' community, and, at nine p.m., the only glow was usually from the streetlights.

Peter greeted us at the door. He was a forty-five year old, 6'5" black man who was built like a bodybuilder with a bald head. He practiced law at Stafford and Herrick on Greenbriar Parkway. We walked in and saw the rest of the party guests. Donald Lascara, forty-five, was the CEO of Lascara and Law on Independence Parkway. He was a Philipino, 5'9" with gray hair, and I'd heard he was good at what he did. Clarence Jankell was a forty-one-year-old African-American lawyer at Jankell and Ireland on Progressive Drive. He was six feet tall with a fade, and his hair was mostly black with specks of gray. Coach Krisby was there, along with Benjamin Parker, who was a white man with brown hair and a clean face. I think he was the youngest at thirty-eight, but he was, also, fat and sweaty. And last but not least was the host, Frank Gregory. Frank was a retired entrepreneur, a sixty-five-year-old impotent, gay man who just enjoyed watching younger men have sex in his bedroom. He owned several gas stations and two Pizza Huts, and he could've lived anywhere but he had chosen the Cottages.

"Our guest of honor has arrived!" Frank announced.

All the gentlemen put their wineglasses down and clapped for me as I stood there.

"Okay, let's get this party started! Everyone pull straws." I waited up against the wall. "And the two shortest straws are…Benjie and Peter! Okay, the backroom is all set up. We'll be out here."

In the room, Mr. Gregory had cameras set up on the closet, the right corner of the wall, and in front of the window. All of the cameras sent our every move to the living room on the flat screen television, where the men watched. We took off all of our clothes and prepared for the show.

I, instantly, felt inferior to the men. They both had broad shoulders and muscular chests. Benjamin had more of a stomach, but they both had monster cocks, and I wasn't too sure my asshole could take it. Fear gripped the pit of my stomach as I saw what was before me. Benjamin looked as if he were more than nine inches. He was hung like some mystical creature I had never seen before! And he must have never touched a razor, because his pubic hair was spread like wildfire over his balls and thighs and even up his stomach.

After I got on my knees, he gripped the back of my head and put the tip of his dick in my mouth. I felt the penis go inside my mouth and slide on top of my tongue. Inch by inch, he forced it deeper into my mouth, and he was so big that it, at one point, got hard for me to breathe.

"Relax, baby. Breathe through your nose."

Because I had no gag reflex, it was easy for me to relax my jaw and throat muscles. Then, he was in my throat, and the tears really came down.

"Shhh, it's going to be all right."

I wasn't crying; I was just tearing up. I looked over, and Peter was on the bed, jerking off, while he watched me get face fucked. Benjamin pulled out of my mouth and helped me onto the bed. I got on all fours and bent over, waiting for the monstrosity to cum inside of me. Instead, I got a warm, wet tongue that danced all around my balls and asshole. His tongue went inside of me and licked the walls of my insides. I moaned. It felt so good that I had to grip the sheets. I looked at Peter and motioned for him to come to me.

"Put your dick in my mouth."

He didn't waste any time. Now, I had a cock in my mouth and a tongue in my ass. Peter grabbed the back of my head, bent down, and said, "I'll be gentle."

And he was. He stroked the inside of my mouth slowly. He was a gentle giant in the bedroom, and I actually took pleasure in pleasuring him.

Benjamin laid down on the bed. "Come here."

I did. I sat on top of his dick in the reverse cowgirl position, and I pulled Peter close to me and took him in my mouth again. Benjamin put his hands on my hips and bounced me up and down on top of him. This made me go faster on Peter's dick. Both men moaned and groaned in ecstasy, stretching my mouth and ass to a whole new wideness. My penis was fully erect, so I reached my right hand down to stroke it. I turned my head and watched us in the mirror. I was turned on at the sight of me bouncing up and down on top of one man's dick and gulping down another's. I jerked harder and faster, and then I came, shooting up so high that my cum splattered my chin and Peter's ball sack. This turned Peter on. He grabbed my hair and shoved deep inside me harder and harder until his load was dripping down my throat and into my stomach. He removed his dick from my mouth, kissed me on my forehead, grabbed his clothes, and left. I was still bouncing on Benjamin when Donald came in. As he undressed, Benjamin moaned, and I could feel his hugeness getting bigger before he erupted inside of me. I rolled off of him.

"Thanks, kid." Donald got on his knees on the bed. I hated being fucked by him because he fucked hard and in one position until he came. He could care less if I got any pleasure out of it.

"C'mon. Turn over."

I went over to him and got on all fours with my ass in the air and my face in the sheets. He stuck it in and got to fucking. I just stared into the cameras, hoping somebody could see my pain. I don't know why I wanted them to see it. I wasn't forced to be there. But there I was, face down in the bed with this monster fucking me—with these men fucking me—lying to their wives about where they were, so they could fuck another man's asshole. Donald pulled out, threw me on my back, and shot his load in my face. Then, he dressed and left.

I felt like a whore. I should have put a price tag on it. At least, then, I wouldn't be broke. I got dressed and looked at myself in the mirror. Ever since I had turned this new gay leaf, my life had completely changed—and not for the better. Who am I? I wondered. I'm not this guy.

"Hey, the rest of the guys were wondering…Why are you dressed?" Frank was standing in the doorway, holding a wig and some women's lingerie in his hand.

"Did you expect me to wear that?"

"Of course! I bought it today. It's your size. Well, I sure do hope it's your size." He held the garment up to me. "Yes, that's about right. Wonderful! Now, get undressed. There are more guests to attend to."

I brushed past him and found Earl. "I'm ready to go."

"What? Why are you dressed?"

Frank stood in the middle of the floor. "Earl, what is the meaning of this?"

"Uh…" Earl looked scared. "Babe, why don't you just go back in the room? Is it the outfit? You don't want to wear the outfit?"

"No, Earl, I don't want to do this anymore."

Frank laughed. "Kid, it is not about you. It is about my investment. I have invested too much money into you for you to just stop and go."

"Earl, what is he talking about?"

"Hmm? Earl, you told me he was okay with it. Seems like you're a bad liar, as well as a bad gambler."

"Look, kid, I—"

"Kid?" I was so confused and was starting to get very upset.

Frank picked up his glass of wine and took a sip.

"Your master here has a gambling problem. He owed some people large sums of money and needed to catch up on his bills. So, in exchange for the funds that I extended to him, he volunteered the ass of his sex slave to the lot of us for one year."

I looked at Earl with tears in my eyes. "Master? Sex slave?" He didn't know what to say and stammered out words that formed no sentences. "Save it. I'm leaving."

"Earl, if he leaves without finishing his year, then I want my money back. And if you can't give it to me, which you and I both know you can't, I will have Donald here take you to court for child molestation, and everyone here can be a witness to it."

Peter put a DVD in the DVD player, and, suddenly, Earl and I were having sex all over the television screen. "And I do have a DVD of you fucking your boy toy. You won't be able to have a successful career—that is, if you make it out of prison."

I looked at Earl, who was obviously scared, and, why I felt remorse for him? I don't know. I picked up the wig and lingerie and walked back to the room.

"Oh, wonderful! The party is still on, people! Clarence and Coach, you two are next, and then we will all go in for an orgy, how's that?"

An applause rang out. "Ooooh, marvelous! I just love these parties!"

For the rest of the night, I did not get an erection. I did not put forth an effort; I did not enjoy myself. I just let them do what they wanted with me, and, at the end of the night, I walked out of the front door and started walking down Kempsville Road toward home.

I was thinking about all of the different things I could do to make Earl's life a living hell when I heard a car slow up behind me. I thought it was Earl trying to apologize, so I didn't turn around. I didn't want to hear another lie from another grown man.

"Hey, stranger."

I looked over, and it was Scarlet driving her car. I guess, even at midnight, you could see the pain on my face, because she said, "What the fuck?" She put the car in park and got out. "What happened?"

I wanted to speak, but I was trying too hard to fight back tears. They came anyway.

"Oh, baby." She held me and just let me cry while she kept whispering, "I'll kill 'em. Just tell me who, and I'll do it."

"Can we go somewhere to talk?"

"Yeah! You wanna go to the Waffle House? There's never anybody there."

I nodded. We got in the car and drove off.

At Waffle House, the bacon sizzled, and the cheese melted, and the smell was enticing. It made me think of my father, who was a great cook. I loved helping him in the kitchen.

"So, who am I killing tonight?"

I looked at Scarlet. It was the first time I had noticed what she was wearing. Her hair was slicked back into a long ponytail. She had on a black cut-up T-shirt that hung off of one shoulder and the tightest red linen pants I had ever seen in my life. She completed the outfit with some black moccasins. I took a deep breath and started from the beginning at football tryouts and continued on up to the present, only pausing when the food was delivered. Scarlet's eyes showed all of her emotions—anger, enjoyment, more anger, and then...

"Well, fuck this shit! Let's go!"

"Scarlet, wait."

"What!"

"First, keep your voice down," I whispered. "Second, what are you going to do? These are lawyers and a very rich man."

"I don't know what I'll do, but I know this ain't right."

I shook my head. "Fuck my life!"

"Don't say that, baby! You fucked up, but you can change it at whenever you feel like it."

"How? If I don't do the parties, then Earl goes to prison."

"And is that your problem?" Her anger was starting to pour out of her eyes. They became red as they pierced my soul.

I tried to explain. "No, but I…I…"

"You better not say you love him! You better not say it!"

"Shhh!"

"He traded you for money! He lied to you. He said he loved you and didn't mean it. He doesn't deserve your love, your remorse, or your compassion. For breaking your heart, he deserves prison!"

I played with my eggs. "What's wrong with me? Why am I letting this happen to me?"

"'Cause you don't know what you're doing. These men assault you, and, when they're done, you see hearts. What the fuck is up with that? Why can't you just yell rape like a normal person?" I laughed. "I mean, just do you. Don't look for a man. This is high school. All you need to do is make A's and go to college. You don't need all this extra stress."

She was right. I was doing too much.

"And another thing. I gave you my number, and yo' ass never called me."

"Oh, well, I—"

"Nope! Fuck you, bitch." I laughed while she pretended to be mad. "But for real, you don't have any friends, and I'm trying to be one, a good one, actually."

I looked at her and smiled. "You're right."

"I know I am. Now eat ya food. I'm not paying for you to play with it."

I never attended another party, and Frank must have kept up with his promise because I never saw Earl again…except for his face plastered all over the news, CNN, and the newspapers. Earl was charged with sexual assault, rape, molestation, and child pornography. I never went to the cops, and I never testified. But I'm pretty sure that the detectives found all of the love letters I wrote him, my clothes in his closet, the pictures of me he took with his phone, and, of course, the videos we made. There was nothing he could say to get himself out of that mess. A week after the next party that I didn't attend, we had a new bus driver. Ms. Kate was her name.

When I told Scarlet, all she said was "Hmm," and then she kept it moving.

CHARLOTTE

It had been two whole weeks, and Jen hadn't replied to my texts or phone calls. I didn't even know why she was trippin'. Must be a young girl thing, I thought. I was mostly shocked at myself. If she had been one of my exes, I would have said, "Fuck her" and been on to the next one. But I truly felt some type of way about Jen. I was in love with her, and being apart from her hurt more than I expected. I remembered the last time my heart had felt like that. It was ten years ago, July 2001.

I had just left the salon I worked at. I unlocked the door and let myself into Kadeem's apartment. I was shocked to see the apartment was actually clean, and I could hear Kenny G on the stereo.

"Hey, baby!" I heard him shout from the kitchen.

I followed his voice only to discover him cooking. "Babe, what are you doing?"

"What do you mean?" He kissed me. "Today is our four year anniversary."

I watched him cut vegetables. He was so handsome, dark-skinned with dreads and brown eyes. He had big soup cooler lips and muscles everywhere you looked. Kadeem loved cooking, and he owned two very lucrative restaurants.

"Well, we usually don't make a big deal about our anniversary."

"I know, but what does that say about me if I can't make one day out of my girl's life special?"

I smiled. "Every day is special as long as you're in it." I kissed him, and he smiled.

"Okay, make yourself comfortable. I'm putting the finishing touches on everything. You want some wine?"

"Nope! Been sober for three weeks!"

"That's my baby."

I went into the living room and looked out of the window, down onto Town Center, where couples were walking hand in hand toward the many restaurants to enjoy their dates. Kadeem stayed in Studio 56 Lofts, and his view was incredible to me. There was no clear view of the sunset and no water to stare at, but there was life. There were people driving east and west and pedestrians walking to and fro. At night, the streetlights and restaurant signs glowed brightly, and my eyes danced from one sign to the next, sucking it all in.

Kadeem came up behind me with a wine glass. "Here you go. Don't worry. It's grape juice. Come on; let's eat." We sat at the table and talked and ate. "You enjoying the food?" he asked.

"Oh, my God, yes! I would love to have you cook for me every day of my life!"

"You know I would love that! Baby, I'd cook whatever you want."

I was drinking the last of my juice when I looked in the bottom of the glass and saw the biggest ring I'd ever seen. I moved the glass from my lips and let the contents fall through my fingers until I was holding the most beautiful diamond ring. I just stared at it.

"What is this?"

Kadeem got down on one knee next to me and took the ring out of my hand. "This is a symbol of my love for you. The ring is the symbol of eternity. Like time, it has no beginning and no end. The hole in the ring is the symbol of the door leading to things and events both known and unknown." He took my hand in his and slipped the ring on my finger. "And I put it on this finger because there is a vein in this finger that goes directly to your heart. That's where I want to be, in your heart."

I looked down at the piece of jewelry that rested on my finger. There were three diamonds on the silver band; the center was one the biggest.

"Charlotte," he said while I looked at him, "will you marry me?"

"Kadeem, I—"

"Look, I know you've been hurt before, and I've tried for four years to be the best man I can be. I just want you to let me be everything you ever wanted and needed. You don't have to answer now; you can take your time." He got up and kissed me on my forehead.

I didn't know what to say. Up until then, I knew I was in love with him, but, when I saw him down on one knee, my heart said, What about Kathryn? I began to feel intense sadness, because as this man smiled and talked to me for another hour, I realized I could never love him the way he loved me, the way I thought I had loved him for so many years.

That night, while he was holding me in bed, I stared at the ring in the moonlight. It was so beautiful, and I felt unworthy of it. I looked at Kadeem. He was wearing a Breathe Right strip, and the sight of that made me hurt even more. A year ago, I had gotten up enough courage to wake him up and tell him his snoring was bothering me. He rolled out of bed and went to every service station and Wal-Mart in the area until he found them. Then, he got back in bed, said, "That should do it," and went to sleep. He was perfect because he only wanted to make me happy, but I knew I couldn't marry him if I was in love with someone else.

A week later, I told Kathryn how I felt about her at Jen's thirteenth birthday party, and she said some hurtful things I'd never repeat. That night, I tried to give Kadeem his ring back and finally left without a word. For a whole month, he called my phone, and I wouldn't answer. I locked myself away in my house and cried myself to sleep every night. I had stopped eating, and, eventually, I lost any energy to get up in the morning. I would wake up before my eyes opened and prayed that they stayed closed. I wanted to murder the sun because it shone brightly on everything good, and I represented everything that was bad. Why was the world still going on when I obviously had become paralyzed by pain and grief?

And that was the same pain I felt, waiting for Jen to reply to my text messages.

"Jen, I'm sorry," I texted her.

She wouldn't reply. I sat down at my computer and tried to do some work. Tick. Tick. Tick. It was nine p.m. Nine p.m.? Where did the time go? I felt like I had just woken up. I looked in the window and could see my sad and pathetic reflection. My afro was matted to my head, and I was completely naked. My excuse was that I didn't want clothes in the way of me rolling over to go use the bathroom, but, really, I didn't feel like putting forth an effort. Ding. Ding. Text message…it was Jen!

The text simply read, "Okay."

Jen

I don't know why I texted Charlotte back. Maybe I was being childish about everything. Relationships are about compromise, and I did tell her I would try the threesome thing one day. Who better than Paris, my best friend? I texted them both and apologized and asked them to meet me at Charlotte's house in Riverwalk. When I got to the house, Paris wasn't there yet, so I talked to Charlotte.

"I'm sorry, Jen. I shouldn't have said what I said nor should I have tried to pressure you into doing something you weren't comfortable doing."

"You're fine. I should've been more open. I mean, you had told me this straight up at the beginning, and I should have known it was coming."

"But you weren't ready. I'm sorry."

I kissed her, just a little peck. "It's okay. I forgive you."

She leaned in and kissed me again, this time longer and with more tongue. I melted like the first time she had kissed me in that fitting room. I didn't realize I had missed her this much. We were kissing passionately when there was a knock at the door. Paris.

She ran to me and hugged me. "Jen, I am so sorry! I would never do anything to jeopardize our friendship."

"You're fine, Paris. In fact, I want to do it...now."

They both looked confused.

"Now, as in right now?"

I looked at them, walked away, and started to strip as I walked up the stairs. "Right now." I took my bra off and dropped it.

The girls followed me to Charlotte's bed, and Charlotte and I helped Paris get undressed. I could tell by the look on her face that Paris was thinking, Oh, my God! Am I really doing this? Here she was, being stripped down by two lesbians. Charlotte kissed me. Then, I kissed Paris. She was shocked. She didn't know what to do, but I did. I grabbed her waist, pulled her close to me, and put my tongue in her mouth. Oh, my God! Paris was a good kisser! It was like her mouth was performing tricks just for me. I was so turned on that I let my left hand slip down lower to grab her sexy ass. She moaned a little, and I knew she was enjoying my fingers caressing her curves.

CHARLOTTE

I was so turned on when Jen put one of Paris's breasts in her mouth. I couldn't take it anymore. I moved in close and helped Jen lay Paris down on the bed, and, while she licked her nipples, I kissed her lips. Damn! Paris can kiss! I thought. I had expected to show Paris some tricks, but her tongue was definitely showing my mouth some.

Jen

Paris was moaning and getting excited, and, as I licked her nipples, I slipped my fingers into her already-wet vagina and then slipped them out and began to play with her clitoris. She moaned heavily, and I couldn't take it anymore. I put my head down by her pussy and began to lick her clit and finger her at the same time. She started humping my face, getting my whole face wet. I knew I shocked her when I went down there. She was trying not to jump and move so much, but she couldn't help it. I knew she had been eaten out before, but not like this. My fingers went deep inside her, and, soon, she was moaning and yelping so much she had to stop kissing Charlotte, who in turn lifted her head.

107

CHARLOTTE

"Watch your friend eat your pussy," I said.

Jen looked up into Paris's wide and excited eyes, and then she started going faster. Paris threw herself back on the bed in extreme pleasure. I leaned down and whispered into Paris's ear, "Is this what you wanted?"

"Yes! Yes!" Paris screamed out. And then I quickly, straddled her face. She didn't have to ask any questions; she knew what I wanted. She began to lick me. I assumed she had never licked a pussy before, but I told her what to do, and she listened. She was such a good listener. She did everything I told her to do, and I gyrated on her tongue for maximum pleasure. Ooh, Paris hit all of my sweet spots. Soon, I didn't have to tell her to do anything. She put her hands on my hips and guided my body over her face. I was approaching my orgasm.

Jen

I heard her about to cum, so I stepped up my tongue game and watched as Paris's and Charlotte's bodies writhed with excitement and pleasure. Charlotte came in Paris's mouth, and Paris came in mine. Both of them screamed together, and Paris was bucking so hard she almost threw

Charlotte off the bed. She was lying on the bed with her eyes closed and breathing heavily when Charlotte tapped on my shoulder. She opened her eyes to see this huge dildo attached to a strap.

"What is that?"

CHARLOTTE

"Well, your best friend has been licking your pussy. Don't you think you owe her a fucking?" She looked at the thing as if I had given her a ten page math problem. "Need help?" She nodded. I helped her into the strap-on and looked at her. She still had that same stupid look on her face.

Jen

She put me on all fours and started licking both of my holes, plunging her tongue deeper and deeper inside me. I was squealing with pleasure, and I looked at Paris, who was getting turned on by the sight of it all. She started stroking the cock as if it were hers and slowly walked over to the bed.

"You want some of this pussy?"

Paris nodded. She kept getting closer until Charlotte moved.

CHARLOTTE

"You better fuck the shit out of her!"

After I put the dildo against Jen's wet hole, Paris rammed it in. I started slapping her ass.

"Harder! Fuck her harder!"

Paris pulled almost all the way out and then rammed it in to the hilt. Jen yelped. Paris grabbed her hips and pulled her into the penis. I could tell everyone was getting turned on. Paris even started talking dirty.

"You fucking whore! Take this dick. Aw, yeah, bitch. You like that?" She was in the zone then. I crawled in front of Jen, spread her legs, grabbed her hair, and forced her face down in my wet mound. Jen was in the middle as we both used her for our pleasure. She was our sex slave. Paris leaned forward and squeezed at Jen's breasts and nipples while she shoved my massiveness into her. I kept Jen's head down while she lapped at my clit like a dog. I could hear Paris driving herself into multiple orgasms.

Jen

There was a rainstorm of cum flowing out of my pussy and onto Paris's dick. She had no intentions of slowing

110

down, and she kept fucking me good while I came. I didn't stop licking Charlotte.

CHARLOTTE

Soon, I was cumming, too. As my shaking passed, we had to beg Paris to stop, and we all collapsed in a breathless, sweaty pile on the bed.

I kissed them both. "Anybody up for a shower?"

Jen

It was five p.m., and Mom wasn't home. Lately, she was getting home later and later, and I knew Pops was going to be out of town, so I called Charlotte. It was Christmas time, and I was definitely in the giving mood.

"Hey, babe."

"Hey, what's up?"

"Well, I have a problem."

"And what's that?"

"I'm horny, and my car is in the shop."

"Hmm, do you want to come here and let me take care of that for you?"

"No, I've got the house to myself."

"Are you sure, Jen?"

"Yep."

"Okay, I'm coming,"

"Hey, remember that fuck buddy you told me about?"

"Yeah, what about him?"

"Bring him," I said right before I hung up.

Boy Toy

Jermaine McCray was the first guy I dated that was close to my age. I was twenty-one, and he was twenty-three. He was a student at Tidewater Community College, and we met when I came home for Christmas break. One afternoon in particular, we double dated with Scarlet and her friend, and I asked her to drop us off a few blocks from my house.

"Goodnight, baby," she said.

"Goodnight," Jermaine and I said in unison.

We walked down the street with our hands in our pockets. He was tall, a little taller than me, and skinny like me. His skin was the color of caramel, just a tad bit darker than me. He was mixed, black and white, and his hair was low cut, which helped bring his facial features out.

"So, I was thinking…you should come to my house."

He hesitated. "But what about your family?"

"They're not home."

I looked up at him, and he smiled. "Okay."

When we got to my house, I noticed that someone had already plugged in the Christmas lights, so we went straight upstairs to my room and shut the door.

Jen

My bed was full-sized and way too small for three people, so I took my comforter down to the first floor, to my mom's office. I checked my phone.

Charlotte had texted, saying, "Open the door."

I opened the door. "Why didn't you just knock?"

"Because...I dunno...I'm nervous. I parked all the way down the street."

"Why?"

"Because, if Kat comes home, I don't want her blocking me in. I wanna be able to haul ass!"

"Where's the fuck buddy?"

"Smoking a cigarette."

I looked out the screen door and saw this big man walking up the driveway.

"Oh, here he is." She grabbed his hand. "Carl, this is Jen. Jen, this is—"

"Coach Krisby?"

Boy Toy

In my room, I turned on some slow music and took off my shirt. Jermaine took off all of his clothes and pulled me to him and kissed me.

113

"Lay on the bed," I told him.

He did. I got on top of him and kissed from his knees to his pelvic bone. Then, I took his penis in my mouth and gave it one long suck, and he let out a deep groan. I licked his stomach up to his chest, where I sucked on both of his nipples. He moaned a little before grabbing my face and kissing me. We kissed as he rolled me onto my back. He sat up and finished undressing me. Then, he straddled my face, and I took him inside my mouth. To my surprise, he leaned down and put my erection in his mouth.

Jen

As I looked at Carl and he at me, both of our faces showed the shock in knowing what had been planned by Charlotte.

She saw the looks on our faces and asked, "How do you guys know each other?"

"Charlotte, he's my high school gym teacher."

"What!" Charlotte yelled, and Coach nodded and looked away.

Boy Toy

"What was that?" Jermaine stopped suddenly, but I pushed his head back down.

Boy Toy

Jermaine's sack was on my nose. He was so deep in my mouth. I could tell he was enjoying being in my throat because he kept stopping my pleasure treatment to moan, and I had to keep putting his head down. I decided to take him on a gay high, so I played with his asshole with my middle finger. I fingered his asshole while he fucked my face and sucked my dick. He was pumping my mouth faster and faster and sucking me harder and harder. I could tell what was about to happen. And it did. Cum was dripping down my throat at the same time cum was spraying the back of his. But neither one of us stopped sucking. It felt so good. I was happy our mouths were filled with cock or surely our moans of pleasure would have rung throughout the neighborhood. He rolled off me and laid next to me in the bed. He held me and kissed me, and we started drifting off, staring at the clock. 6:35.

Jen

Coach was lying next to me on the floor with his hand up my shirt, playing with my nipples. Charlotte's head was bobbing below, and she shocked me when she plunged her fingers into my wet pussy. She began to finger me to the same rhythm she was bobbing her head to. Coach helped me take my shirt off, so he could see my naked breasts out in the open. He pulled out and played with one while he sucked on the other. I watched as his manly hands seemed to enjoy caressing my body. Charlotte stopped sucking him, and he got on his knees in front of me.

His penis was huge. It wasn't long; it was just so wide! And it was in front of my pussy, ready to do damage. I closed my eyes and felt him slowly separate my lips wide open as he slipped inside of me. I moaned as the monster disappeared and reappeared in my vagina. He pumped faster, and his hands happily ran up and down my thin body, caressing my breasts, grabbing at my waist and pressing down on my lower stomach. I was in sex heaven, and I didn't want him to stop, but Charlotte made him change positions.

He sat on the white loveseat that was in the corner, and I practically threw myself on his cock, sighing as I slowly sat on him. I started to bounce, slowly at first and then faster and faster. Charlotte stood up on the chair arms in front of me and stooped down on Coach's face. His hands held her in midair as he lapped at her wetness. Charlotte pulled at her brown nipples and licked them while moaning out her enjoyment. I was bouncing on my front row seat to her road to sexual fulfillment. Every time I sat down on Coach's dick, it was hitting my stomach, causing me to yell out. Between my show and the thick, hard penis inside of me, I was getting turned on and couldn't control the tablespoons of cum that were leaving me and soaking him. I kept bouncing and squishing, and he kept licking, and soon Charlotte was leaking all over his face, and he added his cum to mine, causing a cream pie in my vagina.

I climbed off of him and laid on the floor, breathing heavily, completely drained of energy. Before I knew it, Charlotte was on her knees, ass up, face down in my twat. She was licking the leftover cum out of me, and Coach took the opportunity to get behind her and fuck the shit out of her. I could tell he was hitting her spot because she was making those familiar faces she made with me and making those special noises she only made when she was about to cum. She reached her hand back and started playing with her clitoris. The deeper Coach was in her, the deeper her tongue went in me, and it felt like only a few moments before we all began to hit our orgasms before finally collapsing in a sweaty mess in my mom's office. I took a glance at the clock. It was 7:30. We all held each other and went to sleep.

Kathryn

This particular weekend, my husband went out of town to preach. He would be gone Friday and Saturday and come back Sunday morning in time to preach at our church. I thought it would be perfect to have the whole weekend with my young lover. It was cold outside, and I wanted to make it hot inside. We were at the Cheesecake Factory, outside of Pembroke Mall. The windows were sprayed with fake snow, and there was a ten foot tall Christmas tree in the middle of the store. We had just finished a very delicious dinner. This just made me want to enjoy him more. My husband brought me to the Cheesecake Factory once and then never brought me back again because, to him, it was too expensive, and we weren't "those type" of people.

The waiter came and asked, "Would you like to see a dessert menu?"

"Sure," Robbie said, and the waiter went off to fetch one. "I can assure you that the best dessert is not on the menu." Robbie looked at me, and I smiled.

"My husband is out of town, and the kids are gone. Why don't you come by so I can give you some dessert?"

The waiter handed us each a menu.

"Uh, no, thanks. May we have the check please?"

We pulled up to my townhome at eight p.m. Robbie and I got out of the car and walked up the walk hand in hand.

"Wow, it's dark in there."

I smiled. "That's because nobody's home." I turned the key and let us in. "Well, this is it."

"Oh, you have three stories?" We were standing in the foyer.

"Yes, but I can assure you that everything you need is on the top floor." I took his hand in mine and guided him upstairs to the master bedroom. I turned on the light to reveal my king-sized bed. "You can lay down while I get comfortable." I went into the bathroom, put on my all-white lingerie, and touched up my make-up. I tossed my hair and looked at myself in the mirror. I felt naughty, and I didn't know if it was a feeling or not, but I felt delicious. When I walked out of the bathroom, Robbie was completely naked on the bed. "Let's try something different tonight," I suggested.

"Mmm, like what?"

I reached under my pillow and took out two pair of handcuffs and handcuffed each of his arms to the bed frame. His face showed his uncertainty and discomfort.

"Calm down, baby. I'll be gentle." I climbed on top of him and began to bounce up and down.

José

I was going to leave straight from the barber shop at seven and head to Emporia, but I had plenty of errands to run, and, on top of that, I had left my robe and commentary at the house. I wasn't too pressed because I wasn't preaching that night; I was preaching the next night. I pulled up to the house, and the only light on was the one in my bedroom.

"Hey, Mr. Matos."

I turned to see Tony, Jen's ex-boyfriend, walking up the driveway with a bouquet of flowers.

"Hey! What are you doing here?"

"Well, I need to talk to Jen. I love her, and I need her in my life."

"Pfft, kid, you don't know what love is."

"Actually, sir. Yes, I do."

"Well, if you did, you wouldn't have cheated on my daughter with all of those little girls!" He was quiet. "She's a grown woman who knows what love is. You're a little boy just looking to get your toes curled." I turned the key and let myself into the house, leaving the door open.

Boy Toy

When I awoke from my nap, my penis was in Jermaine's mouth.

"Babe, what are you doing?"

He didn't stop sucking, and I didn't try to convince him otherwise. I put my head back and let myself enjoy.

Kathryn

"You like that, baby?" I was bouncing harder now and enjoying every minute of it. I was just about to cum when the door swung open.

José

"What in the world is going on in here!" I yelled.

The room smelled of sex, and my wife was in lingerie, bouncing on some boy!

All hell broke loose that night. I grabbed Kathryn by her hair and dragged her slutty body off the bed. Then, I looked at the naked boy, handcuffed to the bed, and laid into his hind parts.

Kathryn

"Please! Please don't kill him! José, stop! No!"

He was punching and punching, and poor Robbie was defenseless. I grabbed at my husband's arms, and he pushed me down to the floor.

"Stay over there!"

I cowered in the corner.

Boy Toy

We ran into my parent's room, and Dad was beating some naked guy in the bed. I looked and saw Mom in the corner, yelling, wearing white lingerie.

"Dad, what are you doing?"

He turned around. "Michael, get out of here!"

At the sight of me, his expression turned to despair. He just shook his head in disbelief. "No, no, no!"

I looked down…

José

He had wood. Both of their penises were hard, and they were standing there in nothing but their boxers. The other boy was hiding behind Michael, scared, but the way he was standing…the way he was touching him…

"Michael."

"Okay, Dad. Wait. I wanted to tell you, but I couldn't. I…Dad, I…please—"

Jen

When I woke up, the others were still asleep. I thought I'd have some fun, so I began to eat out my lover. I enjoyed hearing her moan herself awake. When she opened her tired eyes, they locked with mine, and she smiled.

Then, she stopped suddenly. "Do you hear that?"

I didn't hear anything, so I kept going. She leaned back and let me lap at her.

Then, the office door opened, and there was a silhouette in the doorway. "Jen?"

"Tony!"

He flipped the light switch and saw a sleeping Coach Krisby and my face down on Charlotte. "What the fuck?"

"Tony, get out of here."

He shook his head and threw the flowers at me before storming out of the office. I got up to go after him.

Kathryn

As I chased my husband down the stairs, I yelled, "Baby, look! I can explain."

Michael was running behind me. "Dad, can you just wait a minute?"

When we got to the foyer, Tony was about to go out the front door.

"Tony, what are you doing here?" I asked.

"Nothing," he said and walked out. From the foyer, our heads swiveled to the direction he came from, and I saw Jen standing in the hall, naked.

Then, Charlotte came running behind her. "Jen!"

At the sight of our family, she stopped dead in her tracks.

"What in the world?" José yelled.

"What are you guys doing here?" Jen asked.

"What do you mean what are we doing here? I pay the bills here! Ain't this my house?" José yelled.

Then, some fat white man walked into the hall.

MICHAEL

"Coach Krisby?" I hadn't seen him in four years.

"Michael, what are you doing here?"

"You know what? I'm gone," Dad said, and he left us yelling after him while he got in his truck.

"Shit!" Mom yelled. This scared the hell out of me because she never cursed.

"Who is he?" Jen asked, pointing to Jermaine.

"Really, Jen? How about you tell me why you and my so-called friend are butt naked in my house! And who is this man?" Mom demanded.

They were both quiet, and then Fish said, "Kitty Kat, Jen and I are…together."

"Together?" Mom and I said in unison.

The two of them held hands and looked up at us. Then, Mom asked, "So, who is he?"

"Uh, I'm Carl Krisby, ma'am. I taught the kids when they were in high school."

I didn't know why he chose that time to jump into teacher mode. He could have easily said he was a fuck buddy or something.

"So, why are you in my house? In my office?"

Charlotte grabbed his hand and pulled him close to her. "He's with us."

Mom's eyes grew wide. "Fish, this is the last time you screw me over! You brought this man in my house, and you been screwing him—and my daughter, no less—behind my back. What kind of friend are you?"

125

"Mom, really? I'm twenty-three. I'm grown."

"Then, get...out! You graduated from college; you obviously don't need us anymore. Get your stuff tonight and leave!"

"But, Mom—"

I started to speak, but Jermaine grabbed my arm, and I stopped.

She turned and looked at us. "Is everybody a faggot now?"

Jermaine got pissed. "Excuse me, ma'am, but that is very offensive to the gay community."

"Well, isn't that what you are?"

"Excuse me, but, if I'm a faggot, then you're a hoe 'cause ya lil' boy is still tied up upstairs."

Mom swung to slap him, but I moved him out of the way.

"Everybody out!" she yelled before she ran upstairs.

Jen

"Excuse me? Mom had a guy upstairs?"

"I should be going," Coach said.

But Michael stopped him. "I'm pretty sure Charlotte doesn't know, and there's no better night than tonight."

"Know what?" Charlotte asked.

"Please just let me leave," Coach begged.

Michael leaned down and whispered something in his ear. Then, he looked at us. "Coach Krisby was my lover during my freshman year of high school."

Everybody yelled, "What?"

Charlotte walked up to him. "Is this true?"

"Babe, it was before I met you…"

"Save it!" She walked back in the office, and I ran behind her.

Kathryn

I ran into the bedroom, and, upon seeing Robbie, my heart dropped down to my ankles. Tears welled up in my eyes. The poor boy's face was purple and red from the beating. His right eye had started swelling shut, and his lip and nose were bleeding. He was a sad sight, and I begged for forgiveness as I frantically unlocked the handcuffs.

"Robbie, I'm so sorry. Baby, I'm so sorry. He was supposed to be going out of town." I kept repeating my apologies, thinking how emasculated he must have felt while he took his beating from my husband. He climbed off of the bed and grabbed at his chest as he tried to dress himself. I tried to help him put his pants on.

"Get…away…from me," he ordered through clenched teeth.

I backed away from him and watched as he struggled to put his clothes on.

"Robbie, talk to me please." Silence. "I'm sorry, Robbie. I really am. I didn't know—"

"You stood there!" He said as he looked at himself in the mirror while I stood five feet away.

"What was I supposed to do? He—"

"Un-handcuff me? That would have helped a lot, Kathryn!" We stared at each other for a minute. "Don't call me!"

"But, Robbie—"

"Mrs. Matos! Please." Then, he grabbed his coat and left me standing there.

Jen

In the office, as Charlotte and I were getting dressed, she said,

"You can stay with me, so go get your stuff."

I had no problem staying with her. I mean, she was, after all, my girlfriend.

Coach Krisby came into the office. "Babe…"

"Don't call me that," she muttered. She put her jacket on and looked at him. "What kind of sick bastard are you, huh?"

He tried to touch her. "Babe—"

"Don't touch me and don't call me that! How old was he when you did that to him?" Silence. "You don't know, because you don't care, you sick fuck! Jen, get your shit. I'm going to pull the car around."

She started to walk away, and then this stupid man asked, "Are you going to take me home?"

Charlotte turned around and punched him in the face. "Jen!" I jumped. "Twenty minutes!"

MICHAEL

Jermaine and I sat on the couch and watched as Mom's friend left, holding his chest. Jen went up to fetch her things.

"What are you going to do now?" Jermaine asked.

I just looked at him. What else could I do at a time like that? I pulled out my cell phone and dialed seven digits.

When she answered the phone, she was breathing heavy. "Make it quick, babe. I'm busy."

"Scarlet, I really need you."

"What? Nigga, get off of me! Shut up...move! Go ahead, what's wrong?"

I started explaining to her what happened, and, before I got halfway through, she said, "Get your shit," and hung up.

"She coming?"

I looked at him. "Yeah, I'm going to go pack."

He leaned in and kissed me. "I'll help."

We walked hand in hand up the stairs, and I turned and looked at the Christmas tree.

Merry Christmas to me, I thought.

Scarlet

Two weeks had passed, and Michael was still on my couch. I mean, don't get me wrong, I love him, but he needed to talk to his parents and make things right instead of hiding from the conflict and flattening my cushions in the process.

My apartment was small. When you walked in the door, my foyer was a 2' x 4' area of pressed tile. To the left was my living room with a cream colored entertainment center on the same wall as the door and a dark green leather sectional covering the adjacent left wall. Straight ahead was a hallway that led to a guest bedroom, which I had turned into my movie room. A big screen TV was on the wall, and there was a black and gold couch and a love seat to sit on. The furniture was an all-black cloth material with big gold flowers stitched into them. The master bedroom and bath were to the left of the hall, and the guest bathroom was to the right. To the right of the front door was the kitchenette and next to it was my small kitchen. Through the kitchen was my laundry room. It was small, but it was everything I needed, and it was a place I could call my own.

One morning, I made a cup of coffee, hoping the strong smell would wake Michael. He didn't budge. I started frying bacon and then scrambling eggs. No movement. I even started sautéing onions and green peppers for my homemade hash browns. Nothing. Finally, I walked around the counter and kicked the couch.

"Babe."

Michael was lying on the dark green couch in the front room. He turned over, and I could see his puffy red eyes and his sunken-in cheeks. He looked horrible, like life was kicking his butt. He didn't have on anything except a pair of pajama pants, and his hair looked terrible.

"Sit up. Let's talk." He sat up, and I handed him my cordless handset. "Call your father."

"I can't."

"Then, call your mother." Silence. "Call your sister." More silence. "Well, call somebody!" He looked at his hands, and I sat down. "Then, talk to me." I looked at him as the steam from my coffee cup floated up and performed a disappearing act in the air.

He inhaled deeply and kept his eyes on his shaking hands. The room was dim because the only light was that coming from the kitchen. Even though it was just him and me in the room, I felt as if we had an audience. Both of our reflections were in the TV, eagerly waiting to hear what he was going to say.

"My daddy's number one rule was 'if you're gay, don't tell me because I don't want to know.' He acted as if knowing that we were gay would kill him. I mean, I didn't know Jen was gay. And her messing with Charlotte is pretty awkward, but who am I to judge? I was a sex slave to grown men in their forties." He paused a second. "I mean, you should have seen the look on his face when he put the pieces of the puzzle together and realized I wasn't the son he was proud of." He shook his head. "A raging faggot, I tell ya."

"Stop that! Don't talk about yourself like that."

As his eyes filled with tears, he looked into mine. "You didn't see his face. You didn't see the disgust and disappointment that filled his eyes. His eyes were wide with shock, and his mouth twisted in pain as he looked at me…standing there with the boy I had just fucked." He shook his head and looked back at his fingers, eyes filled with tears. "Can you imagine how it must feel to raise your child to be one thing, and they are the exact opposite?"

I got up and got him some tissue. "It's okay, babe."

"No, it's not!"

I jumped at the sudden change of tone.

"My family has been ripped apart, Scarlet! Do you even know what that feels like? No, because your parents have given you everything, and your life is so perfect. You can pick up the phone and call Mr. and Mrs. Waters, and everything is fine! I can't do that!"

My heart began to beat faster from anger. "Oh, is that what you think? That my life is perfect? You don't know shit about my life!"

"I know you're rich and your parents brought you a new car fresh off the lot."

I stood up. "Oh, you know so much, huh? Have you ever seen my parents, Michael?"

He stood. "No, I don't have to see them to know they raised a spoiled brat!"

"Spoiled?"

"Yeah, that's the reason why you fight so much, because you want everything to go your way. And when it doesn't, you go off."

"That's the reason? That's the damn reason, Michael?"

"Yeah!"

"Fuck you! You don't know shit!"

"You're mad because I'm right."

I stormed over to the entertainment center and pulled down a picture frame. "Not that I have to prove shit to you…" I threw the frame, and he caught it. "Those are my damn parents, dumb ass!"

He looked down and saw the picture of me bruised up and beaten up outside the boxing ring with Jack and Brittany on both sides of me, smiling hard. He didn't say a word as I went to my room and came back with the newspaper clipping. I handed it to him and showed him the mugshot of my mother in an article titled "Chesapeake Mother Beats Child Molester Boyfriend to Death."

I pointed to the picture. "This is the reason why I fight all the time. She killed for me and was sentenced to life in prison, and, as soon as she found out that I was with a family that loved me, she committed suicide in her cell." He looked up at me, and I could tell he was looking for words. "I fight because I'm pissed! If I hadn't told her what he was doing to me, she would still be alive. And if she was alive, then I wouldn't have got sent to Mrs. Rainey, who made me abort my baby."

"Scarlet, I—"

"Don't apologize to me. You said what you've been thinking all along." He stared at me. "Lucky for you, today, I'm in a forgiving mood. You can stay; I'm not going to kick you out. But you will respect me and my house, understood?"

"Yes."

"And you go back to school in three days. I expect you to be on that plane."

He nodded. I put the frame back on the entertainment center and took my article back to my room where I shut the door, leaving him standing in embarrassment in the living room.

CHARLOTTE

Jen had been living with me for two weeks. Surprisingly, she was handling the whole situation very well. She had begun performing the role of housewife. In the mornings, she cooked breakfast, and, at night, she cooked dinner. We were undoubtedly becoming closer, and I was very happy. I was upset that her family had to split for us to feel this way, but, all the same, she was that missing puzzle piece that my life needed.

One night, while we were lying in bed, staring into each other's eyes, I said, "I love you."

"I love you, too."

"I don't ever want to lose you."

"You don't have to worry about that. I'm not going anywhere." I smiled at her, and she continued. "Hey, remember when you were telling me about those sex parties and orgies you were having?"

I hesitated. "Yeah."

"Well, how do you feel about…having one?"

I just looked at her for a moment. "Why? Do you want to have one?"

"Well, yeah, I can be open."

"Oh, babe, you don't have to do that."

"Well, I just don't want our relationship to get boring, so…you know."

I smiled at her. "Baby, I think we're fine for a while." We kissed slowly and said goodnight. As I laid there watching her, I realized that I didn't need anyone else in my life—or my bed, for that matter. All I needed was her.

The next afternoon, I gathered my coat, purse, and keys. I went in the bedroom and found Jen texting a friend while she waited for her toenails to dry. She was wearing nothing more than a black tank top and pink lace underwear as she laid back on the bed.

"I'm going to run some errands. You want to come?"

She sat up, and I noticed she wasn't wearing a bra. "No, thanks. I think I'm going to hang out here."

"Okay, love you."

"Love you, too."

While I was out, I called Jen periodically throughout the day, and she didn't answer any of my phone calls or my texts. I didn't think anything of it; just thought she might have had her phone on silent or been napping. I thought I might have been gone for eight hours before I pulled up to my house. To my surprise, there were five cars parked outside.

"I know this little bitch is not having a damn party in my damn house!"

I put the key in the door and listened before turning. No music. I opened the door and instantly smelled sweat. It stunk! All of the lights were out all over the house, except in my kitchen. I walked down the hall and could hear moaning and groaning, but I just kept walking toward the light. Before I could get to the kitchen, I was stopped by the sight of a motherfucking orgy taking place in my damn living room! I wanted to scream, but all I could do was let my mouth drop at the sight of ten different people, completely naked, fucking in my house! And all I could think was, Where the fuck is Jen?

"Hey!" I yelled out. Everyone stopped and stared. "What the fuck is going on in my damn house?"

One man moved back and sat down, and another guy rolled over and Jen sat up. "What's the matter, Charlotte?"

"Oh, bitch!" I started laughing the way I did when I got pissed, and I threw my jacket and scarf down. I marched over to her and tried to slap the taste out of her mouth. The spectators all jumped and gasped.

"What the fuck is wrong with you?" She got up from the floor and, in turn, slapped me.

"Bitch, I know you didn't just put your hands on me!" I took my fist and punched her dead in her nose. She collapsed to the ground, causing my Berber carpet to become drenched in dark red blood. I looked at my naked houseguests. "Now, you sweaty asses, listen up! I am prepared to whoop every ass in this motherfuckin' house! You got sixty seconds to haul ass or have it whooped! Pick one!"

I watched as four women and five guys slowly and nonchalantly started getting dressed, mumbling to themselves. I went into the drawer in the kitchen and came back in the living room. I cocked my gun and shot out a window, causing everybody to scream. "Thirty seconds!"

After that, the people hurriedly threw on their clothes, yelling obscenities before running out of the house. I looked down to see Jen crying on the floor. "Bitch, you better start talking before I kill you!" She rolled over, crying. I had no intention of killing her. However, I was holding a gun, and I was very pissed.

"You said you liked orgies and sex parties, so I threw one. You said I should be more open."

"With me, dumb ass! I wanted you to have orgies and parties with me! Without me, it's cheating! And last night, I told you, you didn't have to do that."

She stood. "But you said you were reluctant to be in a real relationship because your heart was broken."

"I, also, said I would be faithful to you. Last night, I said we were fine. But you did this anyway? This was not about me; it was about you."

By now, she was bawling, and her mouth and chin were covered in blood. I was thinking about taking her to a hospital, but I changed my mind.

"Kathryn would have never done this."

"What?"

I went upstairs and slammed my bedroom door.

Two minutes later, Jen opened it, still dripping with blood. "Kathryn, my mother?"

"What are you talking about?"

"You said Kathryn would never do this. Who's Kathryn?"

I looked out the window. "Who do you think it is?" It was quiet for a while,

"You bitch!" I didn't pay her any mind. "You and my mom dated?"

"No." I went in the bathroom, wet a towel, and grabbed a robe for her. I handed both of them to her. "She turned me down."

"What?"

I sighed and sat on the bed. "She should probably tell you herself, but—"

"No, you tell me!"

"Calm down! I'm about to tell you! Kat and I lived together for years. You know that. And, back in those days, we made love several times." I paused here to give her a

137

chance to soak it all in. "On your thirteenth birthday, I asked her to marry me."

I looked at her to see her staring at me in disbelief. She slowly sat down on the foot of the bed. "But, she was married to Pops. Why would you put her in that position?"

I shrugged. "Because I loved her. I was selfish. I wanted her to be with me forever. She was so beautiful with that long hair and that body that made my mouth water."

She stared at me. "Is that why you're with me?"

"What?"

"Everybody says I look just like her. Did you want me because I remind you of her?"

"You know, I asked myself that every day since the first time we had sex. And, after what just happened here tonight…I can honestly say yes." I got up and headed for the door while she sat there, eyes wide. "I'm going to go get a drink. I'll be back by twelve. I want your stuff out of my house when I get back." Then, I went downstairs, grabbed my coat, purse, and keys, and left.

Kathryn

For two weeks, my husband slept on the cool leather couch downstairs on the second floor, even though there were two empty rooms on the third. My children had packed up their necessities and had moved out, with their lovers, no doubt. I knew José was not going to sleep in any of their beds. I knew I wouldn't. I would walk past their rooms some days and just stare inside, never going in. I couldn't help but remember the day Michael brought home his first girlfriend, or the day when Jen announced that she was going to marry Tony. To me, they were normal children, loving the opposite sex and staying out late, doing God knows what, going to school and bringing home good grades. And if they didn't, they were my children. I was proud to be their mother.

But now, I didn't know who they are. Who was the boy who liked boys? Who was the girl who liked older women? I didn't know these people. I couldn't even imagine the things they had probably done. I didn't even want to fathom my children taking part in such activities. But that was what my family had been subjected to.

I hadn't talked to Robbie since the incident. I knew he needed his space, and it still wasn't time for me to apologize yet. I picked up my cell phone and stared at it. I had an inbox full of un-answered emails from clients, but no missed calls or texts from my children or my lover. I stared at the phone until the backlight went out, and, when it did, I pressed the power button and brought it back up again. I took a deep breath and texted my feelings to Robbie. I knew it was too soon, but I couldn't hold it in any longer. As soon as I set the phone down a text came: "*Robbie does not want to talk to you-www.mrnumber.com.*" Just as I was about to tend to my depression and crawl under my covers, there was a banging at the door. I went down two flights of stairs in search of my caller, and there, in jeans and a brown peacoat and purple scarf, stood Charlotte. I could smell the liquor on her through my screen door.

"Charlotte, what are you doing here?"

"I came to apologize."

"Okay."

"Not for dating Jen, but for bringing a random man in your house, having sex in your house, and keeping it all a secret from you for the past two months."

"You done?"

"No. I messed up. I changed her. She's not the same person I met."

"Ya think?" I let the door slam behind me as I stepped out onto the porch. "The person you met was an infant born in Norfolk General Hospital. The person you dated was a twenty-three year old heterosexual. Now, she's a homo. What did you do to my baby?"

"I'm sorry, Kat. I thought she was feeling me, and I caught her checking me out, so I initiated something. In my mind, she was grown, and it was fine."

I laughed a little and shook my head. "The real reason why you initiated something is because she looks just like me. I was stupid to think you were over that little crush you had on me."

"Little crush? What are you talking about?"

"Oh, please, Charlotte. Don't act like you didn't propose to me!"

"Oh, I'll admit to that, but you said I had a little crush on you. Excuse me, ma'am, but I was and still am in love with you!"

"Even more reason why you went after my daughter." I got in her face. "You are a pathetic little girl. You are forty-six, but you still act like a freshman in college. You used my turning you down as an excuse for not marrying the man you should have. Why won't you stop being a slut and date like an adult? But the real reason why you won't grow up and put on your big girl panties is because you enjoy blaming me for your failed love life instead of taking responsibility of it yourself."

140

"Get out of my face, Kathryn, before I hurt you!"

"Do it!" I didn't budge. We were so close that I could feel her breath in my face each time she exhaled.

"I hate you," she mumbled. "I had you up on a pedestal for so many years, thinking you were so damn special. But you're not, and neither is your slutty-ass daughter."

She turned her back on me, and I kicked her in the middle of it. She fell down all five steps and rolled a little. When she stood up, there was a gash on the side of her head, and dark red blood was dripping down the side of her face.

"Oh, yeah?"

She ran up the steps, and I ran in the house and tried to run up the stairs to escape her, but she grabbed my calf while I was in mid- stride and yanked as hard as she could. I fell and my jaw hit the floor, causing me to bite down hard on my tongue. She rolled me on my back and started throwing blows at my face. She hit me so fast that I didn't know what to do. Finally, I raised my right fist and punched her in her left ear, and she fell off of me, hitting the dining room set and moving it about two feet. We both stood to our feet, and, after swallowing a mouthful of blood, I punched her so hard that she fell back into the wall.

"Get out of my house!"

She wiped her mouth with the back of her sleeve and looked at me long and hard.

"I know you heard me!"

She looked at me for a few seconds more. Then, she left.

I was washing my face in the second floor restroom when I heard the front door open. I stopped moving and could hear my heart beating in my ears. I strained to listen for that familiar sound, and, there it was, the sound of hard soles walking up the steps. José was home. I looked at myself in the mirror and didn't move until I heard him walk into the kitchen and open the refrigerator door.

I walked into the living room, which opened to the kitchen, and walked up to the bar. "Hey, José."

He popped his head up and his face said, "What happened to you?", but, aloud, he just said, "Hey." He shut the refrigerator door and grabbed his keys.

"Wait!"

He stopped. "What?"

"Well…" I played with my fingers. "Can we talk?"

He shifted his weight from side to side.

"*Estoy escuchando,*" he replied.

"Well, José, I am very sorry. I did not mean for you to get hurt. It's just…we're going through the motions of this marriage, but we aren't married." He had a look of confusion on his face. "It's like we're roommates. We sleep in the same bed, and we live together, but where is the love? I know I haven't felt it in years. I met you when you were a senior in high school. The first day I ever saw you was January 25, 1987, remember that? I showed up to your house, and you came outside and opened the door for me, and the first thing I saw was your chest. You were so muscular and big." I laughed a little nervous laugh. "And you grabbed my hand and helped me out of my car, and you picked me up, and I was so shocked. When we went inside, you introduced me to all your family and friends as your girlfriend." I laughed. "And I said, 'José, I am not your girlfriend,' and you said, 'Yes, you are.' And I said, 'You never asked me out.' Remember that?" I smiled, but he didn't.

"Mmm hmm."

"So one night, you got fed up with me telling you that you weren't my man, and you said, 'Look! Either you want to be with me or you don't. Which one is it?' And when I thought about it, nobody had ever asked me out like that. Even though I couldn't stand you, I knew that one day you were going to make me the happiest woman on this earth. So I said yes, and we dated for a year.

I'll never forget when you asked me what I wanted for Valentine's Day. I said, 'Nothing, because I hate Valentine's Day.' And you said, 'No, really, what do you want?' and I told you, 'I want a king-size Snickers and a card.' And when I went over to your house for Valentine's Day, you were so mad because I had showed up in my sweatpants and T-shirt, and you were dressed up, ready to take me out." I laughed and wiped the tears from my face. "I went upstairs to say hey to your mother, and, when I came back downstairs, you had one candle lit and four king-size Snicker bars and a card waiting for me. You stood there, looking at me, and I didn't know what to do, so I said, 'Thank you,' and just stood there. Then, you grabbed me and kissed me, and that was the best night of my life."

He was just standing there as I wiped away tears from my eyes. "I remember when I found out I was pregnant, and you were so happy. You wanted a girl so bad. And you didn't have a job, but you went out the next day, and you found a construction job and made sure we had an apartment by April 1986. My mama and my friends might not have liked you, but you knew when to step up and put me first, and I never said thank you. I might have taken you for granted, but…I love you. I love you, José. And I just want to work this out, please! You are the only person I've ever loved like this, but I feel like I'm the woman you hate—"

"Oh, please! I don't hate you."

"And how can I tell? When was the last time you told me you loved me and it wasn't because I said I love you first or we were about to have sex?"

"Whatever." He started walking toward the door.

"When?"

He walked out of the front door with me staring behind him and went to the truck and got a manila envelope. When he came back in the house, he slammed it down on the dining room table.

"*Yo ya les firmó.* You just have to sign and send them back in, or I'll come pick them up." He started toward the door again. "I did this for you, baby. See, now, you can start some new memories with a new man."

Scarlet

It was ten p.m., and I was banging on my parents' door. Brittany answered.

"Scarlet, what's wrong?" She was standing there in her purple kimono robe with the pink and green flowers. The bottom of the robe danced around her ankles when she walked. I threw my arms around her neck and hugged her.

"Honey, who is it?" Jack came from the back, wearing pajama pants and his navy blue terrycloth robe.

"It's Scarlet, dear."

"Well, what's the matter, Scarlet?"

I grabbed him and hugged him. Brittany rubbed my back, and when I pulled back from Jack, tears were rolling down my face,

"Oh, my baby. Come on." Brittany guided me to the kitchen, and we sat at the table.

Jack poured me a glass of water and sat it in front of me. "Come on, Scarlet. What is it?"

I looked at them both. "I love you guys."

They looked at each other. "And we love you, too," Brittany said.

"You just don't understand how good you have made my life."

"Well, you know, only the best for our little Scarlet."

"No, not just with gifts or boxing." I hesitated. "For years, I thought it was my fault my mother got arrested. I thought that, maybe, if I hadn't told her about those guys, then she wouldn't have killed Marcos, and she would be here with me, and we could have lived together all these years." I looked at them. "But, if I hadn't told her, I wouldn't be the woman that I am today. If she hadn't done what she did, I wouldn't have met you guys. When you adopted me, I finally found a couple who thought I was the most important person in the world. And for that, I thank you."

Brittany had tears in her eyes, and Jack was smiling. "Well, what happened that made you drive all the way over here at this hour?" Jack asked.

I explained Mike's situation and what he'd said to me.

"Well, Scarlet, look at it like this. You went through something that made you a better person, and, while you were going through it, I'm pretty sure you asked yourself, 'Why is this happening to me?' And you probably thought you weren't going to see a brighter day. But it came, didn't it? And that's what Mikey is going through."

"Yeah, baby." Brittany reached out and touched my hand. "Sometimes, you have to go through the storm to get

145

the rainbow. The storm may have broken your windows and blown the shingles off your roof, but, at the end of the day, you're still standing. You're still Scarlet Waters, born in Chesapeake General Hospital on January 18th, 1990. And you are not our Sport."

Both of them had smiles on their faces, and I was still bawling. I wasn't sad at all; I was grateful. There was nothing I could do that would ever make them stop loving me or not forgive me.

Jack and Brittany held me in that kitchen until my waterfall of tears slowed up and I had calmed down. I stayed there that night in my old room.

Jen

When Charlotte finished talking, I was in shock and could not speak nor move. Did she say she was in love with Ma? Oh, yeah, she did, I thought. But what was gut wrenching was the fact that she admitted to dating me because of my resemblance to my mother. Oh, that's fine, I thought. When that front door slammed, I was instantly snapped back into reality. I looked down at my hands. In my right hand, I was holding the bloody, wet towel and, in my left, the robe she had passed me.

In my head, I kept hearing, "You know, I asked myself that every day since the first time we had sex. And after what just happened here tonight...I can honestly say yes." I dropped the contents of my hands and looked at the dresser. I remembered when Charlotte bent over that dresser and let me fuck her for the first time. I walked over to it and looked at myself in the mirror. I looked like something out of a horror movie. Dried blood was smeared all over my face and chest.

I stared into my own eyes and a voice in my head said, "Bitch, she used you because you look like her."

I slapped my reflection's face. Of course, she didn't feel it, and hitting her didn't change her look. She didn't bruise or scar or bleed. She was the invincible, ugly me. I slapped the glass again, and it cracked. We looked at the crack. Then, she looked at me and smiled.

"Is this heifer smiling at me?" I asked aloud. "You ugly bitch, do you know I will kill you!" And that bitch kept smiling at me! Do you know she had the audacity to smile at me as if she was better than me? "Oh, so you the shit now?" I punched the mirror, and, through the cracks, I could still see her ugly face. I kept punching and punching until she disappeared. My right fist was bleeding, and I had shards of glass embedded in my skin. I grabbed the back of the dresser and pulled it over. It hit the floor with a loud crash, shaking the floor.

I looked at the bed. Do you know how many times I had fucked her on that bed? I ran to the kitchen and grabbed two of the biggest knives I could find and went back to the master bedroom. I was breathing heavily. Then, I screamed and began to massacre that queen-sized mattress. I sliced and cut and ripped and shredded that mattress until little bits of padding and springs were sprawled all around the floor. I kicked both of the table lamps, knocking them over and shattering them. Then, I heard laughter coming from the bathroom. I kicked the door open and looked around. I didn't see anyone.

"Over here!"

I looked to the left and saw the ugly bitch in the mirror, smiling at me. She looked even worse than before.

"Look at you! The least you could do is fix yourself up!" She just kept smiling at me, like I was a fucking comedian.

"Am I funny to you? I didn't say anything funny." She kept smiling. "Why are you so happy?" No answer. I walked over to the window and lifted the metal curtain rod off of its posts. I walked back to that whore. "I'm going to wipe that smile off your face." I beat the mirror until she disappeared again. I looked at the curtain rod. The crystal ball at the end had fallen off, and the pole was all beat up. I started to walk out of the bathroom again, but there was that laughter again. I turned around and slowly started walking toward the window.

"Where are you going?"

I jumped and turned. There was that bitch again in the damn mirror! The mirror was eight feet long, and I had only destroyed three feet of it.

I looked at the smiling whore. "I killed you twice. Why won't you die?" She didn't speak. "Answer me!" She just kept smiling. I dropped the curtain rod and beat the mirror down with my fists. I beat it until I couldn't see her anymore, then I looked down at the floor. She was everywhere, all around me, smiling her ugly smile. I began stepping on the mirror pieces with my bare feet, trying to break them, but they wouldn't break. They wouldn't break!

And she laughed and laughed. "You are pathetic!"

"No, you are! Shut up!"

"Make me, Jen." I kept stomping and cutting the bottom of my feet. The more I stomped, the more she laughed. "I am you! The only way I'll shut up is if you shut up."

"Leave me alone!"

She mocked me. "Leave me alone! You're such a baby. If you had any common sense you would have known Charlotte was using you. You're so stupid." She got louder. "And dumb!" And louder. "And fat!" And louder. "And sappy! And naive! And green! And fat! And ugly!" Then, she whispered, "Just… like… me!"

"No! Shut up!"

"Make me!" Her voice seemed to shake the house.

I was scared. I didn't know what to do, but I knew I had to kill that bitch. I couldn't break the glass down anymore, so I picked them up piece by piece and ate them. Then, I blacked out.

CHARLOTTE

I didn't get back home till seven the next morning. I had gone to Applebee's and had one of my favorite drinks: a pomegranate Perfect Margarita mixed with a Jamaican Breeze. Then, I went to go apologize to Kathryn. I don't want to get into any detail about that, but we both started throwing 'bows! When I left her house, I went to Mel's Place off of Indian Lakes and drank until I forgot my name. I blacked out after that, but, at six a.m., some white kid woke me up.

"Hey, miss! You got to go."

I sat up on a bed. There was only a blue light on, and the walls were built of cinder blocks.

"Where am I?" I said softly. I could barely get my voice over a whisper; my throat was so sore.

He tossed my clothes at me. "In my basement. My parents will be home in a couple of hours, and I got to get everybody out... unless you want to help me clean up." I didn't say anything. "Whatever," he muttered, and then he left.

I looked down at myself. I was completely naked. I looked around the basement, and the only other article in there was a camera pointed at me, hooked up to an old television set. I swung my legs over the side of the bed and grimaced in pain. Both of my holes were hurting, and my thighs were so sore. I struggled to put my clothes on, and I looked around and found my purse tossed in a corner. I rummaged through it. Nothing appeared to be missing. I pulled out my keys and started to leave, but, instead, I stopped myself and went to the TV and the camera. I turned both on and hit play.

A white boy appeared on the screen. "So tonight, we picked up this black bitch at the bar, and she agreed to give us all blowjobs. Ain't that right, Kathryn?"

What?

"Yeeeaaah!" The me in the video was so happy and excited. She was talking in a fake white girl voice.

"Well, let's not keep her waiting. Come on out here, boys!"

The basement in the TV was instantly full of teenagers. All of them looked eighteen and younger. I watched as I happily started sucking as many dicks as possible. I hit fast forward. It took me two and a half minutes to fast forward past me giving every guy head. When I pressed play again, I was naked and covered in semen.

An Asian-looking boy came on the screen and said, "Well, Kathryn wants to fuck now."

"Yeah!" I was still in my white girl voice. "Look at my long flowing hair! I'm so pretty!" I was whipping my invisible hair, and the guys laughed at me.

"You have an afro, you stupid hoe!" one guy yelled out.

I fast forwarded for thirty seconds. Play.

"Oh, Kathryn…oh, yes, that's right. Fuck me just like that." Who is that? I wondered. Somebody picked up the camera and walked to the bed. My mouth dropped. It was me! I was on top of some boy, riding him, moaning for Kat!

"What are you talking about? I thought you were Kathryn," one guy said as he laughed.

"Hey! Go get her purse!" another yelled out.

I heard rustling and mumbling. "Charlotte Anne Clemmons. Born…February 7th, 1966! Oh, shit!"

"Damn! She old!"

Then, the bastards held up my license to the camera. They pulled it down and zoomed in on me riding one guy, another guy fucking me in the ass, and another with his dick in my mouth. "She sure doesn't look that old."

I cut the video off and took the tape out. I threw it in my purse and left. When I walked outside, I saw my convertible Chrysler Sebring parked outside. Obviously, I had hit something while I was driving drunk last night, because my left headlight was smashed. I got in the car, started it up, and drove off.

When I got home, I saw that Jen's car was parked in the same spot. I was happy because I wanted to apologize to her. I rushed to the front door. It was still unlocked from when I had stormed out the night before.

"Babe!" No answer. "Jen!" I ran upstairs and went to my room.

It was a disaster. It literally looked as if a tornado had hit it. Blood-covered mirror pieces speckled the floor, and my mattress was completely destroyed. I couldn't even see the floor for all the junk that was on it. I walked into my bathroom, and it was a worse sight. My mirror wall was completely destroyed, and the walls were splattered with little specks of blood. The sink had bloody handprints all over it, and the floor was covered in broken glass pieces and bloody footprints. And stretched out in the middle of it all was Jen.

I rushed over to her. "Jen! Can you hear me?" I picked her up in my arms. Her mouth fell open, and a mouthful of blood poured out. "Oh, no!" I quickly dialed 911, and, within minutes, the paramedics were in my house and putting Jen on a stretcher. "Wait! Is she going to be okay?"

The paramedics felt her neck and then her wrist. "We got a faint pulse! Let's get her to the hospital! Ma'am, are you her mother?"

"No, I'm her…" He stood waiting for my response while the other men rushed her downstairs. "I'm a friend of the family."

"Okay! Well, ma'am. I'm going to need you to call her family. We're going to take her to Chesapeake General Hospital."

"Okay, I'll follow you there." I rushed down the stairs and into my car, and, for three whole minutes, all I heard were sirens and the sound of my heart beating faster and faster.

Kathryn

The automatic doors slowly separated, and I raced through them. I ran up to the nurses' station.

"Jennifer Marie Matos, where is she?"

Before she could reply, I heard, "Kathryn!"

I looked over and saw Charlotte, Michael, and some black girl standing in the waiting room. I walked over to them. "What's going on?"

"Jen attempted suicide last night," Charlotte said.

"What?"

"She ate some glass, and she passed out."

"So why is she just now coming to the hospital? It's 8:30 a.m."

"Well…I didn't get home 'til seven this morning."

"What? I thought you guys were a couple. Why was she left in the house by herself all night long?" My face was full of disgust as she told me what happened the night before. "You had no right to tell her that." Charlotte didn't say anything.

I looked over and saw Michael sitting down with the black girl on his arm. She had long, straight hair that draped over her shoulders and down her back. It was forty-five degrees outside but she was wearing dark blue shorts, black All-Stars that came up over her calf, and a black hoody. Michael was wearing a pair of skinny jeans, some lime green Vans, and a red shirt with Mario hot-pressed on it, and he, also, had on a black jacket.

I sat across from them. "Hey, Michael."

He glanced up at me. "Hey, Ma," he said, and then he looked away.

"Who is this?" I pointed to the girl.

She looked at me and smiled. "Hi, Mrs. Matos. I'm Scarlet." She stretched out her hand, and I shook it.

"So, you're Michael's friend?"

"Yes, ma'am."

I looked at my son. "So, how have you been, Michael?"

He didn't look up. "Good."

"Where you staying?"

"With Scarlet." I looked at her.

"How do your parents feel about that?" I asked her.

"Oh, I have my own place, ma'am."

"Oh, okay. Well, Michael, you know you got your own bed and room at home."

"Got one at Scarlet's, too," he mumbled.

"I don't know why you're being so cold to me. I should be cold to you. You lied to me, and I'm your mother."

"And you lied to me, and you're my mother!"

I just crossed my arms and looked away, but I heard Scarlet whisper, "Stop. You still should respect her."

The double doors on the other side of the nurse's station opened, and the doctor came out and approached us. I stood.

"Hi, I'm Dr. Mullen." He stretched out his hand, and I shook it.

"Hello, doctor, please tell me what's going on."

"Well, I cannot release that information to anyone except a close relative. Are you a family member?"

"Yes, I am her mother." He raised an eyebrow. "Her father is Latino."

"Oh. Well, can we talk in private?"

154

I started to tell him that we were all family there and he could speak freely, but, instead, I said, "Sure."

He led me to a distant corner and showed me some X-rays.

"Well, Mrs. Matos, if you look here, you can see that your daughter ingested plenty of glass. As a result, she cut her mouth, esophagus, and stomach. Now, she has been hemorrhaging for a couple of hours, and the chances of her survival are slim to none. But we're going to do all we can to help her. We need to perform surgery to remove the shards of glass from her esophagus lining and her stomach, but, since she is unconscious, we need to get approval from a family member. This is something usually discussed by both parents. Is your husband here?"

My husband? José? Where is he? I wondered as I said, "No, go ahead with the surgery."

He flipped through the papers of his clipboard. "Okay, I'm going to need your signature on this consent form, saying that you give permission for Chesapeake General Hospital and me, Dr. Mullen, to go ahead and perform the surgery." I signed. "Thank you. I'll be back to give you the report on how the surgery went."

I watched as he walked away and then scurried over to Charlotte.

"What did he say?" she asked. I gave her a briefing. "Did you call José?"

"I called him for thirty minutes, and he didn't answer. I know I left, like, five voicemails." I looked at Michael. "Did you try calling him?" He made a face. "Well…" There was nothing else to say. Of course, they didn't talk. Nobody in the family was speaking to one another.

We sat in the waiting room for hours, eating fast food, watching the news, and watching the clock. One time, when

Mike and Fish went to make a food run, Scarlet and I got a chance to talk.

"So, how did you meet Michael?"

She looked up from her magazine. "I can't believe that he never told you about me. We met his freshman year of high school in the library after school."

"Oh." Scarlet nodded and went back to reading. "Have you guys ever...dated?"

She laughed. "No. Even then, he was...special."

"Ugh!" I looked away. I thought this was some little phase he was going through. But he'd been gay since he was a freshman in high school? He was twenty-one now. It was not a phase, and it was disgusting.

"You know, I don't see a problem with him being gay."

"Well, you're not his mother."

"No, but, I'm the one he talks to, and I know how he feels about everything."

"Hmm." I looked away.

"Well, I'm glad. He, at least, knows that I love him."

"Excuse me? How do you think I feel? I did not raise him to be a faggot."

She threw down her magazine and leaned forward. "Don't call him that!"

"And why not? Isn't that what he is?"

"No, he's gay, not a faggot."

"What's the difference?"

"The difference is you're annoying and a bitch, but there's only one classification that is politically correct and only one I should say out loud. But I can see right now that I'll have to make an exception."

"Who are you talking to?"

"The worst excuse of a mother I've ever seen."

"Little girl, you don't know me."

"Oh, I don't? I know your favorite color is pink; you own your own printing business; Michael is your favorite child, and you don't have many friends. Your best friend is now your daughter's lover, and you were obviously unhappy with the man who pays all of your bills and supplies all of your meals, because you have been messing around with someone your children's age, somebody who must have claimed he loved you and could do so much better, and you stupidly fell for it. You and I both know he can't fill all of your high maintenance needs." She sat back in her chair.

"My son talks too much."

"No, he said just enough. And from what he tells me, I'm happy he's living with me and not a bunch of people who stopped loving him because he's not the same as they are."

"I love my son."

"And how does he know that?"

"What do you mean? My son knows that I love him. I'm just mad at him. I can't be mad?"

"Well, he doesn't think you're just mad." She crossed her legs and picked the magazine back up. "You haven't called him in two weeks."

"And he hasn't called me either."

"Who's the parent? Who's forty-five?" She raised an eyebrow without looking my way. "Hmm?"

We didn't speak anymore. Dr. Mullen came out a little past three, and we all stood.

"Surgery went fine. We removed all of the glass and stitched her back up. She's still under anesthesia, so she won't be awake for a while, but you can see her. Because of the cutting of her esophagus, her throat will be swollen for some time. Her stomach was cut too, so, for the next few weeks, she will be on a liquid diet, with the exception of applesauce, yogurt, oatmeal, and other similar foods. Now, we would like to keep her here for a couple of days for observation, and we have scheduled for a psychiatrist to come see her tomorrow afternoon. Um, again, you can see her, but, if she does wake up, remember that she is to get as much rest as possible. At this time, we are only allowing two people at a time to come in the room. Will that be you and your husband?"

Oh, my goodness! I was so embarrassed. I didn't know where José was, but I knew where he wasn't. "No, my son and me."

I turned and waved for Michael. He, in turn, motioned for Scarlet to come with him, and she whispered something to him. His face was so upset, and she leaned in and kissed his cheek. Their foreheads touched, and she whispered something again.

"Wow! How long have they been dating?" Dr. Mullen said.

"They're not; he's gay."

He got up, and we followed the doctor through the double doors and walked down the hall. We were surrounded by a sea of sickness and death. The doctor pulled back the curtain. "We're going to move her to a room later."

When I saw her, my mouth dropped. She was wearing a neck brace, and the color was completely drained from her face. Her wrists and ankles were strapped down to her bed, and the only proof that she wasn't dead was the beeping of the heart monitor in the corner.

"Now, she's wearing a neck brace, so she doesn't move her head and so her esophagus can heal. And since she attempted suicide, she has to be restrained because she is now a danger to herself." He looked around the room. "Well, I'll leave you." Dr. Mullen left, and the tension in the room was very thick.

Neither of us had seen each other in what seemed like forever, and now we had been drawn together by this tragedy. I turned her hand over, and her fingertips and her palm were so cut up, and skin was peeling off in thick layers. The sight brought tears to my eyes.

Michael broke the silence when he said, "I'm glad she's all right."

"Yeah."

"Well, I'll leave, so Sis can come in."

"Please, don't."

"Why not? That's her girlfriend; she should see her."

"Can I have a few minutes alone with my daughter?" Michael put his head down. "Thank you. And why are you rushing off? You need to stay here and support your sister."

"Support her doing what? Is she entered in some race to see who can get healed faster?"

"Can you please just stay?" He stood in the corner and folded his arms, and then he looked at the clock. "Is there a problem?"

"Naw."

"Doggone! I never thought I'd have to beg for us to be a family."

"You don't have to beg. We ain't one."

"Okay, Michael! You want to leave? Leave!"

And, with that, he was gone.

Scarlet

At the hospital, Michael went to go see his sister for less than five minutes, and then he was storming through the doors again.

"Let's go!" he yelled as he kept walking through the waiting room toward the car.

I got up and looked at Charlotte. "It was nice to meet you!" I said before I ran off behind him.

The ride back to my place was a long one. Neither one of us uttered a word, and Mike was obviously infuriated. His face kept twisting in the most gruesome expressions, and he was breathing heavily with his arms crossed. He still didn't speak to me once we got to the apartment. He just went straight to the bathroom and took a shower.

While he was in there, I decided to call my father. "Hi, Jack."

"Hello, Scarlet."

"Hey, I'm really feeling frustrated right now. Jen, Mike's sister, is in the hospital, and nobody's been able to contact her father all day."

"What?"

"Yeah, and I just don't know what to do. Mike's all upset, and Jen really needs her daddy."

"Okay. I'll handle it."

That was one thing I loved about Jack. When I had a problem, he wasted no time in handling it.

After his shower, Mike went into his room and shut the door. I didn't know what to do. I didn't know how he was feeling. I just knew he needed to know everything was going to be okay. I knocked on his door, but he didn't answer. I turned the knob and went in. I had gotten rid of the two couches that were in there and had brought Mike a bed and a dresser off of Craigslist. He was lying on the bed with his right arm behind his head and his left leg bent up. His towel covered his private parts.

"Two more days, huh?" He didn't say anything. I climbed in bed next to him. "You okay?"

"No. I don't want to be this way."

"What way?"

He just looked at me. "You know what I'm talking about."

"Gay?"

"Yes, gay."

"Well, if you don't like it, change it."

"How?" He looked at me as if I were the stupidest person in the world.

"How do you know you're gay?"

"What do you mean, 'how do I know?'"

"How do you know?"

"Well, I…I…"

"Are you attracted to men?"

"I guess so."

"Are you attracted to women?" He just stared at me, and I climbed off the bed. I looked at him. "Do you find me attractive?"

"Scarlet—"

I took off my shirt, and he was quiet. I dropped it. "Well, do you?"

161

He was speechless as I unbuttoned my shorts and let them fall. I stepped out of them and looked at him. I was standing there in nothing but my pride and fingernail polish. I made my way to the bed.

"Scarlet, wait."

I stopped, and we made eye contact. Then, I slowly pulled off his towel, revealing a very erect nine inch penis. I sat on the bed and touched his arm, then moved my face toward his. Mike tilted his head down toward mine and met my lips with his own. He wrapped his arms around me, and I gently took hold of his torso, resting my hands right below his ribs. We kissed softly at first, once on the lips, twice…he caught my lower lip with both of his and kissed it. Our mouths opened, and his tongue entered mine. I practically fell all over him, and he kissed me deeply, over and over again. His hands began moving over my body, up and down my back, drifting a few fingers over my fat ass.

I explored him, too, touching his back muscles, his abs, his pecs, his arms. His penis was poking me a little. Mike pushed me back on the bed and was on top of me. He looked down at my thin, brown body, and his hands started going crazy, squeezing, gripping, and pinching. I loved it all; he loved it all. He kissed down my neck, nibbled at my shoulders, kissed around my breasts, and flicked my nipples. He kissed down my stomach, his hands following him, unwilling to leave my perky boobs alone. He kissed around my belly button and then mounted me.

In his lust, he was not gentle. His penis entered my tight, wet pussy hard. Mike's weight was above me, and he was forcing his dick into my pussy. Inch by inch, it went in, and my pussy expanded to receive him. I gripped the bed sheets tight as his balls slapped up against my ass. He started pulling out, and I exhaled loudly. Then, he pushed back in, hard, pulled it out slowly, then shoved it back in. Finally, we had a rhythm going, and wet, dirty noises filled the room as our bodies mashed together. His rhythm picked, up and, soon, we were sweating. I scratched his back as he pulled my hair. He forced himself so deep into me that I could feel him hitting my uterus. It hurt so bad, but it felt so good!

"Michael! Michael!" I screamed out.

"Aw, yeah! Cum on my dick!"

I was shocked at his dirty talk, and it turned me on, especially when he said, "I'm about to cum."

"Oh, yeah, baby! Cum!"

"Oh, Scarlet! Oh, Scarlet!"

We gripped each other's backs as I came on him, and he came in me. He stayed inside me for a few extra minutes before leaning over me and kissing me softly for a long time. Something magical happened to the both of us that day. I'll never forget it or regret it.

José

It was a Saturday, and I was at the barber shop, cutting hair. It was around 3:30, and my shop was packed. I was cutting a head when a tall, thin white man walked in. He sat down and picked up a magazine. I didn't say anything to him because I assumed that he was waiting on one of my other five barbers. As the people began to dwindle away, the man was still there. He sat with his legs crossed, wearing khaki pants and a blue dress shirt with a grey and black sweater vest over it. His hair was neatly combed over his head and not a follicle was out of place. Clearly, he wasn't there for a haircut.

"Hey, *mi hombre*! Who you waiting on?"

"You, sir."

"All right, you're next." I quickly cut Elmo's hair and sent him on his way.

The man got up and stretched his hand out to me. "Hi, I'm Jack Avery, Scarlet's father. Can we talk for a minute?"

"Sure." I led the way outside, wondering what he wanted to talk about. I automatically assumed he was there to say that my son had gotten her pregnant, but, recently, I learned my son wasn't into the girl thing. "I'm sorry. Whose father are you?"

"Scarlet. Scarlet Waters?" My face showed pure confusion. "She and your son have been friends since high school."

"Oh, okay."

"Well, she came to my house last night, crying about the situation with you and your family. It had upset her greatly because Scarlet loves Mikey. Now, you may not know our Scarlet, but she speaks so highly of him and talks about him so much, it's like he's an unseen member of our family. But the truth of the matter is, we're not his family. You are. And I came here today to ask you if you might give him a call. He really wants to speak with you."

I took in a deep breath. "Well, Mr. Avery, that all sounds good, but I'm not talking to nobody in my family...any of 'em, especially not my wife."

"Well, I can understand that."

"Thank you. I didn't raise my son like that. You're a father; you can understand. I have kept my family in the church and have spoken nothing but the Word in their lives since they were born. Now look at them. My wife is sleeping around with a boy, my son is doing God knows what with a boy, and who knows what my daughter is doing? But I do know one thing. I'm getting a divorce." Jack's face showed shock. "Yeah."

"But...what about your family?"

"What family? You must not have been listening."

"Yes, I have, sir. But, you are a man of the cloth. Surely, you believe that you were given this family for a reason." I gave him a look. "Or maybe somebody prayed for a closer family. That prayer itself will surely bring conflict into the house."

"In Matthew 19:3-9, Jesus explained to the Pharisees why some divorces were allowed under the Law of Moses and under what circumstances divorces are permissible for Christians. Moses permitted them to divorce their wives because their hearts were hard. But it was not that way from the beginning. Jesus said that anyone who divorces his wife, except for marital unfaithfulness, and marries another woman commits adultery. Now, *mi esposa*, committed 'marital unfaithfulness.' Therefore, I am getting a divorce!"

"Sir, will you please consider calling your son? He has been hiding this for six years. Doesn't that tell you something?"

I was about to say something, but his phone rang.

"I'm sorry. This is my daughter."

While he was on the phone, I was thinking, Six years? My son has been hiding this from me for six years? What kind of father am I that my son can't come to me and talk to me about anything? I mean, I was mad because of how I found out. I thought I had done something wrong as a parent. Obviously, I had if my son couldn't tell me about his sexuality.

Mr. Avery hung up the phone. "Mr. Matos, do you have your cell phone on you?"

"Yeah, it's in my pocket. Why?"

"Your family has been calling you all day. Your daughter is in Chesapeake General. She had surgery today."

"What?" I pulled out my phone. I had twenty-one missed calls from Fish. "I've got to go." I ran into the shop, grabbed my keys, hopped in my truck, and sped to the hospital.

The whole time I was driving, I kept asking myself, What happened? Why did she need surgery? Why didn't I answer the phone? I called Kathryn. No answer. I parked my car in the clergy spot and raced through the sliding door.

"Jennifer Matos?" I inquired.

"She has been moved. She's in Room 339. Go out that door, to your right, go straight down the hall, and you'll run into the elevators."

I said my thanks and ran down the hall toward the elevators. There were four of them, and I smashed every up button. Four elevators, and none of them came down fast enough. When the doors finally did open, I hopped in and pressed the three, and the door close button. I think that was the longest elevator ride I'd ever taken in my life! The doors opened again, and I ran out looking for 339. 301. 305. Wrong way! I ran the other way. 330. 332. 334. Other side. 335. 337. 339, J. Matos.

I knocked on the door, and I heard Kathryn's voice say, "Come in."

I opened the door and slowly walked in. I didn't even see Kathryn. My eyes darted across the dimly lit room and went straight to the bed. My firstborn child was laid up with her eyes closed. I was scared. No man wants to see his child like that. Her face was full of make-up. I was sure Kathryn had everything to do with that. The room was quiet, except for the man in the news on the TV. "So, what happened?"

"Where were you?"

"*¿Lo que está hablando*, Kathryn?"

"What am I talking about? We called you a million and one times, and you didn't answer. Where were you?"

"Where do you think I was? It's a Saturday. I was at the shop."

"So, why didn't you answer the phone?"

"What do you mean why? I don't want to talk to you."

"Well, don't you think, if we called you that much, it must have been an emergency? Fish even left you some voicemails!"

"Well, I ain't get them. And I'm here now, so now what? What you want me to do?"

She grabbed her purse and coat and stood up. "I signed those papers. I'll drop them off at the shop tomorrow."

"Okay."

"I hope you're happy!"

"I am!"

She stormed out. I ran after her. "Are you going to tell me what happened?"

She walked back to me. "Your daughter attempted suicide last night. She tried to eat glass and die. Thankfully, she survived. You would have known that had you been here at 8:30 this morning."

She turned and left. I think I stayed for two hours, and, before I left, I prayed for my baby.

Jen

I'm all better now. I had to undergo plenty of therapy, and I couldn't talk for weeks, trying to heal. I moved back in with my mother. Pops had moved to a small apartment somewhere I'd never been. Michael was back in school, and I guess you could say my family was still divided. I hadn't talked to Charlotte since the incident. Well, she did come by the house after I was able to talk. I remember I was in my room, writing in my diary, when there was a knock at my door.

"Come in."

She walked in wearing black leather tights and a purple sweater dress. "Hi."

"Hey."

"May I sit down?"

I moved my feet back, and she sat at the edge of the bed.

"Jen, I never got to apologize for what I said to you. I didn't mean any of it—"

"You sure about that?"

She looked down before saying, "Well, maybe I did. But when I saw you on that floor, you were all I thought about, not your mother. And I didn't say 'poor Jen.' I said, 'Oh, my God! Look at my wife on this floor.' My wife, Jen. I know that I was meant to be with you. I was attracted to you because you favor Kathryn, but I'm in love with you because you're Jen."

I was sitting on the bed, taking in all her bullshit, when she got down on one knee and pulled a ring box out of her coat pocket. "Sometimes, in life, we make mistakes in who we decide to spend the rest of our lives with. Sometimes, we think we know better than God on who our soulmates are. But, in all actuality, He picks the perfect people out for us, and we turn them away. Well, I'm sorry for turning you away." She took my hand. "Will you marry me, Jennifer Marie Matos?" She put the biggest ring I had ever seen on my finger. It had three diamonds on a silver band, the center one the biggest. I stared in disbelief as the sunlight played with it on my finger. "Well?"

I looked in Charlotte's eyes. I loved the ring, but I didn't love the girl. I took the band off and looked at it in my hand and that was when I noticed something on the inside—something she obviously hadn't. I picked it up and looked closely. Inside, engraved on it, were the words *Love Always, Kadeem*.

"What is it?"

I handed her back the ring. "Sometimes, God does send you the right one. And sometimes, you push them away and try to make it up with somebody else. But I'm not that bitch."

She saw the engraving and then looked at me. I saw her mouth trying to form an apology.

Before she could, I said, "Get out."

And she did.

So, I guess that was it. In the beginning, I started out as a simple girl with normal curiosities and a normal family. Now, I realized I was just finding me.

A sneak peek at…

Once Upon

A

Secret

A Modern Un-Fairy Tale

Nikole

"Oh, I'm sorry," I said as the cute professor and I reached for the tongs at the same time.

"Oh, no, Ms. Turner! You go right ahead," he said.

"Professor Lions, I told you to call me Nikki. I'm twenty, not forty," I said, smiling as I placed some salad on my plate.

"Well, Ms. Turner, no matter how old you are, a man should talk to you with respect."

I smiled. "I'll remember that," I said as I walked toward my table in the Hampton University café.

He was watching me. I didn't have to turn around to know that. I'm gorgeous, and I know it, I thought. Everyone knew it. With my long golden hair, light gold complexion, gray eyes, pink lips, and 125 pound frame, I got approached by guys on an hourly basis, and girls complimented me all of the time.

Last year, I was a sophomore, and I didn't know how to make good grades. Yeah, I'm smart, but college was a little overwhelming. I had brought home one A, two Bs, a C, and two Ds. I'd only had one male teacher, and I flirted with him whenever I saw him; that was how I got one of my Bs.

So, this year, I bought all formfitting clothes, and I made sure all of my teachers were men. Professor Lions taught my Psychology 203 class, where I sat in the first row, with my skirt high and my cleavage out.

I think I started fucking them after midterms; I had one B, two Cs, and three Ds, and I knew I couldn't take that home. So, one day, I approached Mr. Phillips, my Strategies for Start Up teacher, in his Buckman Hall office.

"Mr. Phillips?" I knocked on his door and saw he was on the phone. "Oh, I'll come back later."

After I turned to leave, I dropped my keys on "accident." I knew my skirt was way too tight as I seductively bent over to pick them up.

"Oh, I've got to call you back!" he said before hanging up the phone. "Nikki! What can I do for you?"

I stood up and turned around with a bright smile. "Hey, Mr. Phillips!"

"Hello."

"Umm, I got my midterm grades back."

"Uh huh…"

"And I have a D in your class."

"That's right."

"Well, I was wondering if there was any extra credit I could do to help my grade."

"I'm sorry, but no."

"No?"

"It's in your syllabus. I do not give out extra credit. My class is easy. Just do the work and pretend like you're trying to learn, and you pass."

I threw myself down on the chair in front of his desk and pouted. Tears came to my eyes as I said, "But I am trying. It's just…I can't keep up."

Mr. Phillips stared at my thighs, and I pretended not to notice that my skirt had slid up so far that my panties were showing.

"Mr. Phillips?"

"Oh! I'm sorry, Nikki. I lost my train of thought."

"Mr. Phillips, I'll do anything. I need an A in this class."

Usually when a person says she'll do anything, I thought, *it's pretty much understood that that is not true*. So I really was not expecting what happened next.

My teacher shut his office door and sat in the chair next to me. "I don't give out extra credit, but I do give out bonus points."

"Oh, my God!" I jumped up excitedly. "How can I get those?"

He looked me up and down and licked his lips.

"Well," he started.

"Well?"

"What are you willing to do?"

"I mean…whatever," I answered nervously.

"Hmm…you tell me what you want to do." He stared at my legs as he rubbed his right thigh.

I looked at the door to make sure it was shut. "I don't want anyone to…find out about this."

"About what?" he smiled.

I got down on my knees in front of him and looked up in his face. Then, I unbuckled his belt, undid his pants, and pulled out the fattest penis I had ever seen. I looked back up at Mr. Phillips and asked, "How much will my grade go up if I do this?"

"I'll let you know when you're done."

And with that, I took a deep breath and shoved the whole thing into my mouth. I had never sucked a dick before, but I had seen a lot of women do it in the pornos I'd watched. As I gripped the shaft with my right hand and sucked really hard on the head, he moaned. I moved my hand up and down and bobbed rhythmically. Then, I removed my hand and put my head down as far as I could until I gagged.

"Oh, yeah," he said.

I spat on it and continued to jerk it off. Then, I slowed down and sucked his balls. I beat his dick with my tongue. As I put the head in the back of my throat, I hummed. He really liked that. I kept going until I could feel him growing in my hand and mouth. I sucked his head and beat his dick as hard as I could. Then, at the perfect moment, I stopped sucking, and he shot his cum on my face. I kept jerking him off until his entire load had been released. After giving my teacher one last suck, I looked up at him. His head was tilted all the way back, and his eyes were closed. I had heard that guys got turned on when they saw their cum on girls' faces, so I sat at his feet and waited.

"Was that your first time?" he asked.

"Yeah," I said.

He exhaled deeply. "I could tell."

"Wh-what?"

He lifted his head and looked down at me. "Umm, you don't want to keep that on too long; it's going to be hard to get off." He pointed at my face. Then, he sat up straight and said, "Uh, excuse me." I stood up and got out of his way. He handed me some tissue. After fixing himself back up, he asked, "What's your grade now?"

"A D," I answered.

"Right. You have a C now."

"A C?"

"I'm actually being generous."

"But I need an A!"

"Then, you're going to have to earn it. Either in the classroom or in my office."

"Wait...I have to do that again?"

"If you want the bonus points," he said without even looking at me.

I felt like a slut, a whore, a prostitute...worthless.

"Is there anything else I can do for you?" He asked when he finally looked at me.

"No," I said as I grabbed my purse and left.

The walk back to McGrew Towers was longer than usual as I thought about what I had just done… for a C! I had definitely thought that was A material or, at the very least, B material.

In the lobby, I waved to the RA, got on the elevator, and went to my room, 501. After I let myself in, the first thing I saw was my half-naked roommate.

"Yasmine, where are your clothes?"

She was wearing what looked like a tube top. It had just enough fabric to cover her breasts.

"Don't be mad at me! I didn't know you were going to be here! I thought you were staying at Lonnie's house."

Lonnie was my boyfriend, and she was right; I had told her that I would be staying at his house for the weekend.

"Yeah, I might go over there later," I said as I sat my things on my bed and then sat at my desk. "But I've got to handle some things first. I got my midterm grades back."

"Oh, Lord. What did you get?" She asked. After I handed her my grades, she exclaimed, "Nikole! What is wrong with you? See, I know what it is. It's 'cause you don't get yo' butt up and go to class!"

Even though she was fussing, I laughed. I could not take her seriously without pants on, and, when she got excited, her thick Macon, Georgia accent came out extra strong.

"So, I went to Mr. Phillips and tried to get an A."

"Oh, Lord! Nikki, you can't ask for one; you have to earn one."

"Well, I did more than ask."

"Oh, Lord! What did you do?"

After I told her about everything that had just happened, her mouth dropped to her breasts as she exclaimed, "Nikole! I can't believe you did that!"

"Yeah, and he only gave me a C!"

"What did you think you were going to get? You got to give up the cupcake for an A!"

I checked my email while she continued to rant.

"Oh, my God!" I yelled, shocked.

"What?" she asked.

"All of my teachers want to see me."

"Hmm…I wonder why," she said sarcastically.

"You don't think Mr. Phillips told, do you?" I asked.

"Nikole! Yes!" Yasmine yelled.

I exhaled deeply and set up times to meet with them all. I was getting my things together when my roommate asked, "You're not going like that, are you?"

I looked at myself in the mirror. I still had on the too small clothes.

Before I could answer, she said, "No, you're not! Go and put some sweatpants on!"

I laughed. I loved how she was so concerned.

"For real, for real! You don't need to go. But you ain't gon' listen to me, are you? Nope. Do you need to go in the 'treasure chest'? Yes, you need to go in the treasure chest." She hopped off the bed and opened the drawer that was underneath it. She pulled out a small, decorated box and opened it. It was full of Lifestyle condoms.

"Yasmine, who can fit in these lil-ass condoms?"

"Girl, all condoms are the same size, except Magnums. Nobody can fit a Magnum. Nobody's penis is that big."

"What? Who told you that? Lonnie wears Magnums."

"Mmm hmm." She shook her head. "He lyin'. Take these." She handed me a handful of Lifestyles.

I laughed, put them in my purse, and said, "Okay."

The first teacher I went to was Professor Anderson, my theatre history teacher, in Armstrong Hall. I knew she wouldn't want any favors. One, because I had a B in her class and, two, because she was middle-aged and Caucasian. I'm pretty sure she couldn't even fathom the idea of same-sex sex.

"Hey, Professor Anderson," I said as I walked in the office she shared with Mrs. Jones, another theatre professor. I looked around and saw that we were alone.

"Hello, Nikole! You weren't in my class today."

"Oh, yes! I'm sorry. See. What had happened was—"

"Uh huh," she said, knowing a bad excuse was coming.

I laughed, "Doc. Aye! I'm sorry. I'm just a little overwhelmed."

"Okay...and you have good grades, but you're always either severely late or not present at all."

"I know..."

"And you know, after you miss three classes, you start to drop one letter grade per absence?"

"Yes, ma'am."

"Okay," she said, picking up her attendance book. "So, according to this...you should have failed my class." I just stared at her. "But I didn't put that in, and you have a B."

"I appreciate that."

"Well," she said. Then, after a pause, she said, "Shut the door." I immediately became nervous as I closed the door. "I have a cousin who just graduated from college with a bachelor's degree in film and directing. Now, for some reason, he wants to direct porn. Unfortunately, he doesn't have enough people to get his business off the ground."

"Umm, okay..."

"Well, I will give you extra credit if you work for him as a PA."

"A production assistant?"

"Yes," she said, and I laughed.

"Oh, my goodness…I thought you were going to say something else."

"Oh, no, I would never suggest something that horrid. Well, here's his number." She handed me a business card. "Call him ASAP!"

"Yes, ma'am."

"Okay. That's it."

"Okay. I'll talk to you later, Doc. A."

"Alright," she said.

I left her office, walked down the steps, turned the corner, pushed open the door, and headed to Elmo's office. Elmo was my professor for two classes—Financing New Ventures and Creativity, Innovation, and Product Development. I walked in, and, before I could say hello, he said, "Shut the door, Nikki."

I did.

"Phillips told me what you did."

My heart dropped.

"I have no intention of telling anybody about it; but you have a D in my class," he said as he unbuckled his pants and pulled out his penis. "Now, you can either suck your way to an A, or I can fuck the shit out of you, and you won't ever have to attend another class."

"I could run right now."

"But you won't. You'll be known as the HU slut, and you'll have to tell your parents how you thought this was a good idea. I'm sure they'd love to hear that."

I froze while looking at him.

Immediately, I panicked. *What if I get pregnant by this grown man?*

My teacher pulled out of my vagina, and I could feel his cum running down my thighs as he sat down in his chair. I couldn't move. I didn't know whether to cry or throw up, so I just stayed bent over his desk.

Elmo slapped my ass.

"Good job, Nikki." He let out a sigh. "That's an A for Financing New Ventures."

I turned around and looked at him, confused. "What? What about my A in Creativity, Innovation, and Product Development?"

"What? You didn't think that covered two classes, did you?"

My mouth dropped, and he laughed.

"No, no, no…you're going to have to do that again. And, next time, you need to convince me that you want to do it." As tears ran down my face, he said, "Aw! Don't cry. You wanted this, remember?"

I nodded.

"Yeah…I hate to kick you out, but I do have to get ready to teach a class."

I didn't move.

"Here. I'll help you with your clothes." He pulled up my thong and pants all at once, leaving me uncomfortable. "Okay?"

I nodded. Then, I left.

X

THE NOVELIST

ZION IS A RECENT GRADUATE OF HAMPTON UNIVERSITY, MAJORING IN THEATER ARTS. IN 2011 A PROFESSOR TOLD HER SHE SHOULD WRITE A STORY AND A RECENT BREAK UP GAVE ZION A LOT TO SAY. PEN MET PAPER AND A STORY WAS BIRTHED. IN THE PROCESS OF WRITING HER FIRST MANUSCRIPT, THE STUDENT DISCOVERED SHE WAS WITH CHILD. THIS MOTIVATED HER EVEN MORE TO FINISH HER STORY AND GET IT PUBLISHED. ONCE THE MANUSCRIPT WAS COMPLETE AND THE SEARCH FOR A PUBLISHER BEGAN, THE YOUNG AUTHOR WAS RUSHED TO THE HOSPITAL. SEVEN DAYS LATER SHE GAVE BIRTH TO A DAUGHTER SHE NAMED ZION. TWO HOURS LATER, ZION PASSED AWAY. THIS LOSS CHANGED THE AUTHOR FOREVER, BUT IN THE MIDST OF IT, SHE DECIDED WHENEVER SHE WAS ACHIEVING GREATNESS SHE WOULD GO BY THE NAME OF ZION.

21st Street Publishing

More titles from the 21st Street

Publishing Group…

Sold exclusively on our website,

www.21StreetUrbanEditing.com

&

Amazon.com

www.21StreetUrbanEditing.com
orders@21StreetUrbanEditing.com

21st Street Publishing

www.21StreetUrbanEditing.com
orders@21StreetUrbanEditing.com

21st Street Publishing

Name_____

Address _____

City _____   State_____ Zip _____

__ Dirtiest Revenge by ChaBella Don	$14.99
__ 21st Street: Straight Outta Zompton	$14.99
__ Meet the Jordans by Jen Booth	$14.99
__ Stupid & Love by Charae Lewis	$14.99
__Loyalty Is Everything by John Auletta	$14.99
__Self Pub Guide by Niccole Simmons	$12.99
__Money by Jack Onasis	$14.99
__Twisted Obsession by Vonnie Coates	$14.99
__Alani's Bigger Hustle by Kai Storm	$14.99
__Alani's Hustle Gets Bigger by Kai Storm	$14.99
__Evenings of Score by Doni Matlock	$14.99
__Fast Lane by Shakeera Frazer	$14.99
__The Don Divas by Keisha Howard	$14.99
__Reaper by Glen Pitts	$14.99
__Once Upon A Fling by Zion	$14.99
__Once Upon A Secret by Zion	$14.99
__Absolute Will by Robin Tremly	$14.99
__You Just Don't Know by Kai Storm	$14.99
__ _____	$14.99

Write in title here

We have several new releases coming as well as other titles not listed.
Get on our mailing list for updates.

Please include $2.99 for shipping. We accept checks, money orders and
USPS stamps via mail. Credit card, debit card and Paypal are accepted
online.

Mail orders to: 21st Street Publishing
PO BOX 637
Zion, IL 60099

www.21StreetUrbanEditing.com
orders@21StreetUrbanEditing.com

21st Street Publishing

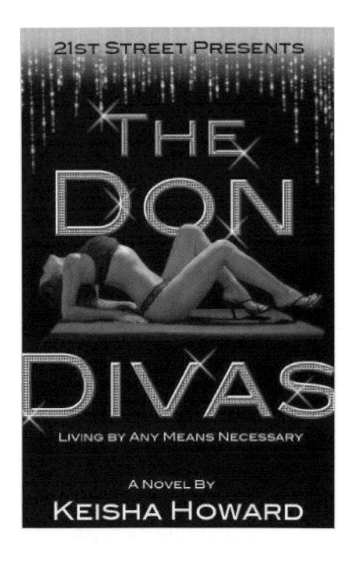

www.21StreetUrbanEditing.com
orders@21StreetUrbanEditing.com

www.21StreetUrbanEditing.com
orders@21StreetUrbanEditing.com

21st Street Publishing

www.21StreetUrbanEditing.com
orders@21StreetUrbanEditing.com

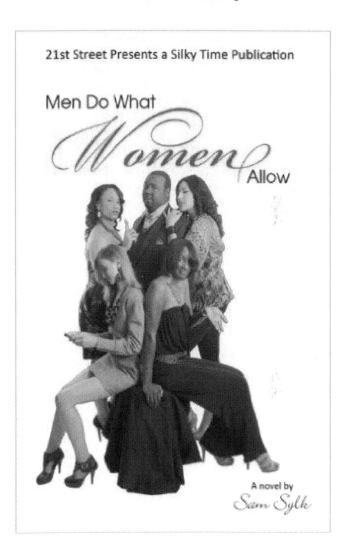

21st Street Presents a Silky Time Publication

Men Do What Women Allow

A novel by
Sam Sylk

www.21StreetUrbanEditing.com
orders@21StreetUrbanEditing.com

21st Street Publishing

FAST LANE

Every Road Has An End.

21st Street Presents a novel by

Shakeera Frazer

www.21StreetUrbanEditing.com
orders@21StreetUrbanEditing.com

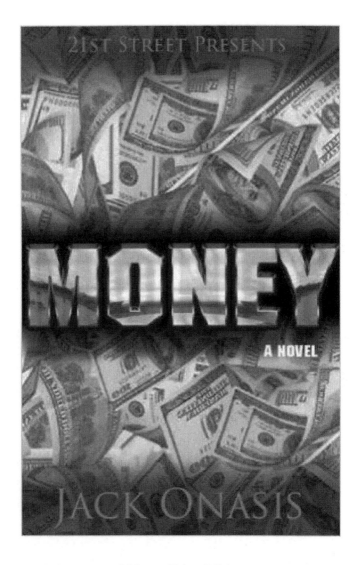

21st Street Presents

MONEY

A NOVEL

JACK ONASIS

www.21StreetUrbanEditing.com
orders@21StreetUrbanEditing.com

21st Street Publishing

www.21StreetUrbanEditing.com
orders@21StreetUrbanEditing.com

21st Street Publishing

www.21StreetUrbanEditing.com
orders@21StreetUrbanEditing.com

21st Street Publishing

21ST PRESENTS A PUCCI PUBLICATION

LOYALTY

IS EVERYTHING

A NOVEL

JOHN "JERSEY" AULETTA

www.21StreetUrbanEditing.com
orders@21StreetUrbanEditing.com

21st Street Publishing

Self Publishing Guide For Urban Fiction Authors

Niccole Simmons

www.21StreetUrbanEditing.com
orders@21StreetUrbanEditing.com

21st Street Publishing

www.21StreetUrbanEditing.com
orders@21StreetUrbanEditing.com

www.21StreetUrbanEditing.com
orders@21StreetUrbanEditing.com

21st Street Publishing

21st Street Presents a 23/1 Publication

REAPER

Glen C. Pitts

www.21StreetUrbanEditing.com
orders@21StreetUrbanEditing.com

21st Street Publishing

Once Upon A
FLING
A Modern Un-Fairy-Tale

ZION

www.21StreetUrbanEditing.com
orders@21StreetUrbanEditing.com

21st Street Publishing

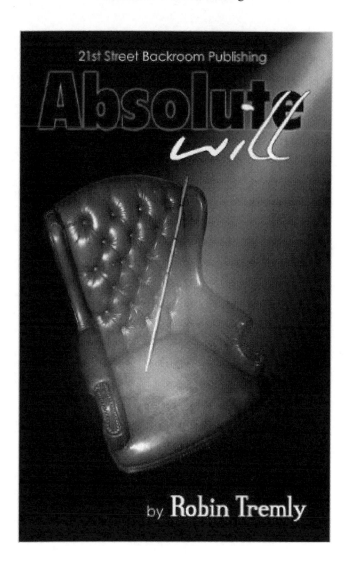

21st Street Backroom Publishing

Absolute
will

by Robin Tremly

www.21StreetUrbanEditing.com
orders@21StreetUrbanEditing.com

Made in the USA
Columbia, SC
20 June 2017